THE HOLMESIAN
BOOK CLUB

ACT I

JL CORDONNIER

TO THE FRIEND, WHO WAS WITH ME SINCE THE BEGINNING.
THE LORD WAS THE ONLY ONE THAT MADE THIS POSSIBLE.

CONTENTS

ACKNOWLEDGEMENTS

PROVERBS 3:6 IN ALL THY WAYS ACKNOWLEDGE HIM, AND HE SHALL DIRECT THY PATHS.

The root of this book and every area of my life is the Lord. Without His inspiration, guidance, patience, and power, this project would not be possible. He set me up with the right people, gave me my muses, and gave me the strength to finish this work. I thank the Lord for its completion and everyone who helped make this possible.

My biggest supporters are my parents. Who never wavered in their encouragement. My dad, who gave me business advice, helped me dust myself off in rough patches, and modeled for Linda in the illustration as her dead body. My mom, in showing me *Little Women*—where Jo March taught me how a book was made and how it could be done—inspired me to write stories and plays of my own. My mom has been my biggest cheerleader and has suffered many of my rants telling her every possible way this book could go until I narrowed in on the right story. My Heavenly Father and my earthly parents have been my anchors through every season of my life.

Muffie, for being an anchor to me as well and showing me love in a dark era. She is the only inspiration given her actual name in the book so that she will be immortalized on the page as in my heart.

Lydia Taylor has been my best friend since childhood and the chief inspiration for the character of Lila Greene. Her loyalty, her encouragement, her bangs, her individuality, her RN mom, and also a long sufferer of many of my ramblings.

Lily Prus, a friend who was partial inspiration for Lila. Also endured many ramblings and gave me an outlet in the earliest stages when I was still figuring what I wanted to write about.

Hunter Sammons, my cousin, and inspiration for the character of Memphis Moses. Though mellowed out now, I'll never forget the times you nearly got us kicked out of the mall or all the mischief we got into as kids.

Frederick "Jamie" Sammons, my cousin and godfather for loosely inspiring Memphis's father, Capt. Wyatt Moses.

Rev. Joe Hill, a real life mentor and inspiration for the character of Rev. David Pike.

All of my childhood bullies inspired the role of Elle Gonzales. Here's a version I wish was true, with an ending I wish had been for us. I didn't like your personalities as kids and we didn't get along, but the Lord has given you all gifts to someday use for His purpose. I pray for God to touch your lives as He has mine.

To my time at an unnamed place for encouraging my love of books, letting me work in a magnificent building, giving me an actual book club, and extensive history that inspired bits and pieces of the mystery of Barry Beaumont.

My muse, the inspiration behind James. The reason this book took an extra few years to complete was because James's character was so difficult to craft. I juggled between making him a security guard, a magician, a cop, a PI, to giving him a mustache or a leather jacket, making him sunshiny and kind or heroic and naive, or just taking him out completely. My muse came just at the right time and set the tone of the finished product.

Vivian Blevins, my creative writing teacher in college. Encouraged my creativity, printed a short story of mine in the newspapers, and was the first to call me a published author.

My friends, family, and church family for modeling as references for the illustrations. Brady and Nikol Hill, Melissa May, Brittany and Paul Haver, Dakota Arrington, and my dad.

Also, to my beta readers who encouraged me, motivated me, and whose feedback finalized the process. Brady and Nikol Hill, Josie Hill, Melissa May, Brittany Haver, my parents, and Jessie Stewart.

My friends and followers on social media. I hope you enjoyed it as much as I did creating it, and that it was worth the wait.

Megan Prado, my editor. A special thanks for going over my draft and putting the finishing touches on it.

Renée Tamsin, my editor, publisher, and friend. I truly believe God intended for us to meet and I couldn't ask for a better person to mentor me. You've helped me develop my voice, sat through draft after draft, spent hours helping me brainstorm, saw potential in an amateur's scribbles, gave me space to explore my creativity, and took a chance on me that many wouldn't take. Here's hoping we'll be the next CS Lewis and JRR Tolkien!

Finally, Sir Arthur Conan Doyle for creating Sherlock Holmes, my ultimate muse. When I decided to make writing my ambition, I didn't know what I'd write about. I liked Nancy Drew and Scooby-Doo as a kid, but I never would've had the courage to pursue mysteries unless I'd found Sherlock when I was 18. He is the root of detective fiction and has inspired innumerable scientists, doctors, police, even basketball players, young people, artists, and writers before me. In his lifetime, Doyle admitted to hating his creation which he thought took away from more important pursuits, but I hope this series will be my life's work. I pray I see but a small fraction of the impact Doyle had. These characters and stories have been so healing for me and I can't wait to see where they go.

"LIFE IS INFINITELY STRANGER THAN ANYTHING WHICH THE MIND OF MAN COULD INVENT."

- SIR ARTHUR CONAN DOYLE -

PROLOGUE

"Do you think we could get in trouble for this?" It was a dumb question. Of course we would.

I was looking at my friend, Lila, when I asked but Memphis snidely interrupted, "With our parents or with the ghost?"

"Ghosts don't exist." Lila's freckled nose scrunched up.

"But ghosts are half the fun," he retorted.

My best friend, my cousin and I had gone to the park before my parents took us out for ice cream. While my parents went to walk around downtown, run some errands, we were told to stay in the ice cream shop until they got back.

Mom worried as she always did but Dad said, "She's almost a teenager now, Faye. We can trust her." He gave me a reassuring wink as they made their way to leave, though Mom looked over her shoulder just as the door closed. As if she knew they shouldn't have left us alone.

Across the street from the shop was the old hotel building. It had been shut down for years and our school had an assortment of rumors about it. We couldn't resist checking it out for ourselves to see if those rumors were true.

"I know there's a ghost in there, but you won't catch me sneaking around. I'm not that stupid," a snotty voice chimed in. Elle ate her orange cream sherbet at the table beside ours.

"Yeah, we're going to miss your fun company…" Lila muttered under her breath before looking at me again, "Should we do it?"

"As if Jenny is brave enough," Elle commented again.

My face turned hot and I sucked in my jaw. The thrill of danger, the idea of getting away with something, and now schoolyard taunts; the perfect storm to get middle school kids to try something really dangerous.

"Can we, Jenny? Can we, please? I wanna check it out!" My cousin's hazel eyes turned as round and innocent as he could make them, like a puppy dog begging for a piece of bacon.

I put a finger to my lips and hummed, thinking for a while until I replied, "The game is afoot!"

My childhood hero's words came out, overriding whatever apprehension the possibility of a ghost may have stirred. Cartoons, films, and books of every kind--needless to say, my obsession with Sherlock Holmes was a pretty prominent part of my personality.

It was just a quick trip, right? Just across the street. It wasn't like I was all alone. Just a quick peek inside to see if it was haunted, then we'd go right back to the shop before my parents knew we were gone.

"You guys are really dumb for this. I hope the ghost gets you." Elle told us while we ventured out of the shop.

What was it in people that made us curious from an early age? The urge to explore and uncover secrets? Go places that were strictly forbidden? Even if it was scary or unsafe, there was something in us that wanted to discover the truth—even at the risk of our lives.

Our impulsivity leading the way, we crossed the street to the condemned building. White paint chipped off, and whatever glass wasn't broken had graffiti sprayed over it. The aged sign over our heads read, *'Cook & Connell Hotel. Est. 1910.'* The first *C* was crooked, threatening to fall off, and the '&' symbol was missing, replaced by a dusty outline.

Although there were bright orange cones surrounding the entrance, it did little to deter three kids who easily bypassed them and headed for the main doors. We pressed our little faces against the glass, squinting into the room to try and get a peek, but it was too dark inside.

"Over here!" Memphis pointed to an open window. He hurried over to it and then motioned for us to follow him.

"Do you wanna do it?" Lila shrunk back, her shoulders rising in a bashful way as if she could hide her face with them. She looked at me, chewing her lip to hold back her grin.

I guffawed, "Yeah!"

We took a quick look around, making sure the coast was clear before we helped each other climb in. Before I followed, I glanced over my shoulder and saw Elle still in the ice cream shop, her eyes wide and her mouth slack. I couldn't help but smirk. She always terrorized me back in school. I bet she'd never expect me to be brave enough to do this. *I'm braver than her,* I thought to myself. That was for sure.

With a shove and a grunt, I made it through the window. When my feet hit the floor, a cloud of dust rose around us and caused us all to cough. It wasn't as dark on the inside as it was on the outside.

"Wow..." Lila looked up. The overhead skylight let the sun in, showing us our way. The glass roof was divided by iron rods that made these geometric patterns like a glowing diamond in the ceiling. Even if a couple of the panes were broken and dirty, it was still beautiful.

"I feel like I'm in ancient Rome." Memphis went to one of the columns holding up the second floor, laughing at the old carvings at the top and bottom of the off-white post. He held up his arms, showing off his muscles with exaggerated growls as if he were Hercules standing in victory after killing a great beast.

"Shh, be careful! We don't want to get caught," I giggled, with equal parts anxiety and excitement, and looked around. My eyes wandered over to some spray paint on the side of the column. Some hobos or gangs must've broken in too.

They're all gone now though...right? I was pretty sure we were alone. At least, I hoped we were.

"Check this out!" Lila went to the opposite wall, finding an old elevator. At least, that's what I thought it was. Behind the open door was a great big metal box. It looked more like a furnace than an elevator, "Want to go upstairs?"

"Not in that thing." I shook my head as I chuckled nervously. When the other two started heading for the stairs, my stomach did a flip, "Maybe we've seen enough. We should go before my parents get back."

"One more minute, one more minute!" My cousin waved a dismissive hand, flying up the stairs, two at a time, without bothering to grab the iron railing on his way.

"Memphis, wait!" I looked down, carefully stepping over the black old wires that trailed over the dusty tile flooring like snakes. When I made it to the stairs, Lila and I followed him.

The more I saw of it, the more this place looked like a haunted house from Sherlock or an episode of Scooby Doo. Floral wallpaper peeled off the top halves of the wall with decades of dead bugs sticking to the backs of it like fly paper. I cringed away, turning closer to the others, just in case a spider or two was lurking in some of the cobwebs that decorated every corner.

"More artwork..." I looked at some graffiti on the floor that read in black, *'Go home.'*

"Ow!" Echoed a couple of feet away from me. When I turned then I saw my cousin rubbing his fluffy blonde head and standing beside a low-hanging chandelier that was slowly making its way to the ground, "Lighting stuff..."

"That girl back at the ice cream shop was wrong. There's no ghost here," Lila almost sounded disappointed, spinning around to take in the whole view.

"Wait, wait. D' you hear that?" Memphis paused and held a hand to his ear.

I made a face, "Stop messing with us. It's not haunted."

"I'm serious! Shh!" He shot us a look.

The two of us clamped our mouths shut at the same time. He was right. I could hear a male voice not far from us, echoing the hotel. Was it downstairs, where we just were? Or was it on this floor? I couldn't tell. I thought back to the graffiti I saw. What if we were never alone? What if a stranger was squatting here and we just woke him up? What if there *was* a ghost?

Lila started to stray further away from the stairs, then she let out a soft gasp when she backed into something. She turned around to see what it was and we all screamed. Before us was a white figure, standing roughly at our height. A white, stoic man with a mustache and a suit. His blank eyes stared down at us, his colorless skin chipping off. It was a bust statue, on a matching white and crumbling pedestal.

The eroded plaque at the base of the statue read, *'Barry Beaumont.'* We shouldn't have screamed so soon. What came next was infinitely more terrifying.

"There you are," a male voice growled, "Get over here!"

There were sudden footsteps. Coming up the stairs. Was it a stranger? A cop? Were we in trouble? Our instinct was to hide. We found a dusty sofa with stuffing coming out of ripped holes–perhaps little homes mice had made over the years–but we could either hide behind a dirty couch or let the man find us.

We held tight to each other, bracing for what was to come. I squeezed my eyes shut and I quietly prayed that the man wouldn't get us, *'I'm sorry, God, for sneaking in here. Help us get out of here without getting caught, and I won't do it again!'*

Our backs pressed tightly against the wall. The footsteps got closer and closer until they stopped. Where did they go? Where did the man go? After what felt like an eternity, I opened my eyes and looked up, only able to see the ceiling. I couldn't hear anything. I couldn't see anything. Until–

The man erupted from the other side of the sofa, glaring down at us before reaching both hands in our direction. We screamed again as we were yanked up to our feet. When we got a better look at him, we realized the man who caught us wore a police uniform. My eyes landed on a name patch that read, *'MOSES.'*

"Uncle Wyatt!" I said with both surprise and relief. I took in his features, his tan skin, a scruffy beard, short spiky brown hair, and laugh lines around his hazel eyes. I was so glad it was family and not a ghost.

"Dad, how did you find us?" Even in the low light, I could see Memphis's face turn beet red.

"Jen's parents got back to the ice cream shop, saw you weren't there. Some girl told 'em you came here. And who d'you think they thought to call for a delinquent breaking-and-entering incident? You know you're not supposed to be in here. What were you three knuckleheads thinking?" He led us back downstairs and briskly out the door.

"Do you have any idea how dangerous that was?! What if you'd been kidnapped?! What were you thinking?!" Uncle Wyatt's professional reprimand couldn't hold a candle to the scolding waiting for me in the car. My mom ran her hands down her face, shaking her head in disbelief.

I turned my face to the window, trying to hide how often I scraped my hand over my wet cheeks. Every time I sniffed, I could still smell rust and mold. At least we were far away from downtown. I didn't want to risk Elle seeing me. I shouldn't be surprised she told on us. I wrestled with feelings of betrayal, relief that it was my uncle who found us, and guilt that I had put my friends and myself into what turned out to be serious danger. What a rotten day this had turned out to be.

"Okay, calm down. Yeah, it was stupid but they've already been told it was wrong and they're not going to do it again. We just can't exercise more of that trust we mentioned earlier..." My dad gave me the side eye before continuing, "You're grounded for the rest of the weekend. No TV, no computer, no going anywhere, but for right now...happy birthday."

He reached over and plopped a box into my lap.

"It's what we were picking up from the post office earlier. We ordered it from the museum's gift shop in England."

I blinked up at him in surprise. Mom seemed understandably hesitant–I probably didn't deserve a birthday present. She opened her mouth to object but my dad just shook his head, warning her not to say anything more.

I looked down at the white box on my lap, stamped with blue and red patriotic graphics. The seal had been broken, and inside was just an ordinary brown box. With burning curiosity, I tore open the box and pushed away the red tissue paper inside to find a tweed deerstalker. A replica of the one worn by Holmes himself.

"Good thing you did this before you got the hat. You might've gotten it dirty." Dad smirked as if there was some part of him that was proud. "Shouldn't have been surprised with where you ended up. Our little detective."

CHAPTER 1
ORIGINS OF A BOSWELL
7 YEARS LATER

"Welcome, everybody, to Wax & Ink! Historically known as the Cook & Connell Hotel, we celebrate the building's 115th anniversary, as well as our first full year of operating the Wax & Ink Bookstore here on the ground floor." The manager's voice echoed throughout the lobby.

"Excuse me, excuse me..." I murmured, squeezing through the crowd of tourists who blocked my way to the mahogany shelves. These days, I don't have to break into the building that used to captivate me as a kid. Who knew I would end up working here as a bookseller?

The old hotel went through some huge changes last year. New wallpaper was put up, a swirling floral seafoam print with brown half-wainscotting underneath it, trailing along every wall. The flooring was replaced with fresh tile, and an overall life was brought back that I had never known before. The place used to haunt my nightmares from that birthday break-in all those years ago, but that was long forgotten. The place and the people were different now.

Dodging my boss's gaze as he continued with his tourist speech, I pulled my phone from my pocket with a shaky grip.

"Whatcha doing?"

I nearly dropped my phone, snapping my head toward the owner of the familiar voice: Lila. "Don't do that! I was looking at something..."

"Has that publisher guy gotten back with you yet?" She tilted her head and playfully lifted her brows.

"That's what I'm checking now."

Her white sneakers squeaked on the floor as she shuffled over. Once she was beside me, we scrolled through my emails.

Monday, 10:30 am
From: michaelmint@mintpublishing.org
To: jenevieveweston@email.com

Miss Weston,

Thank you for submitting your work to Mint Publishing. Unfortunately, we're unable to accept your manuscript at this time. You've shown clear talent in the short stories we've published before, but your writing does not work as a full-length novel. The details feel flat and researched rather than fully formed and portrayed. The leading characters felt one-dimensional and stiff, like high-schoolers putting on a play.

My advice is to find the right story for your voice before adapting it into a long form story. If you can rework this piece in a more immersive style, then I'll give it another look.

Best wishes and good luck,

Michael Mint.

My brows knitted together and I reread the email a couple times to see if I read that right. When I processed that this was a rejection, it was like my stomach fell through the floor. I heaved a sigh, my shoulders slumping forward in defeat. I'd been looking forward to his email all day. I thought this was it for me, that I could start my journey to becoming a novelist. After years of perfecting what was to be my big debut, my book was now back to square one.

"Man, that is brutal." Lila frowned and awkwardly rubbed my arm, "What are you going to do now?"

"I don't know..." I replied numbly.

"—we have Isaac and Helena Carlyle to thank for helping fund the building's reconstruction. Now, if you will all follow me to the second floor, I will let you in on the legend of the spirit of Barry Beaumont..." Mr. Gonzales took his group up the main staircase, leaving us alone in the lobby.

I reached for my cart, pulling it back to my side after the crowd had separated us. I grabbed a couple of books from the top of it and resumed shelving new releases. When would I see my own books on these shelves? The likelihood was dwindling.

"Maybe it's a sign I should just quit," I adjusted one of the books so the colorful cover would stand out to potential readers walking past.

Lila gave me a wincing smile, "I think you're being too hard on yourself. Have you considered some kind of new hobby? Something to take your mind off of the novel thing?"

"Like what?"

Lila ran a hand through her auburn hair, pushing her choppy bangs out of her eyes.

"I mean, I dunno. You've just had tunnel vision lately. Maybe you should see if there's a new project you can do–like knitting or something here at work or whatever you want."

Finishing with the new releases, I started back toward the checkout counter, pushing my wooden cart down the black-and-white tiled flooring, the wheels squeaking in protest as they hit every groove. I released a labored breath at the mere thought of deviating from my writing. How could I do that when everything around me would just pull me back to the pen? Going past grecian columns, study tables, the fireplace, the large print room, the grand staircase with a wooden railing and black rod iron support beams, and of course the new release bookshelves of varying genres.

"So you keep telling me but my only problem is, I don't know what that would be." I steered my cart back behind the front desk, "I appreciate the advice, though. Are you going to buy that stuff?"

Lila held up a couple of books she'd gathered when I wasn't looking, "Oh! Yeah, yeah."

I smirked when I saw the titles. She hadn't changed a bit. All the books were about chemistry, geology, and biology. When I finished ringing them up, I handed them back to her, "Speaking of hobbies, are these for pleasure or those extra courses you've been taking?"

"The first option." Lila put the items into her satchel of personality. She took it with her everywhere and I've come to find it could hold almost everything. It was an indie aesthetic in a color between olive and beige, almost a military bag in fashion. It had a couple of patches on it where Lila had mended holes over the years. Buttons decorated the top of a record, the Union Jack, and a sunflower.

Lila was always unapologetically herself. I envied that about her, how comfortable she was pursuing whatever she wanted.

"I don't know how you can juggle all those courses on top of nursing school."

Lila shrugged and readjusted her bag over her shoulder, "Doing pretty well. So, it's nice to try a couple other things to keep me challenged."

Her casual approach to over-achieving blew my mind. Maybe it's what made us such good friends; complementary differences, but similar in all the ways that mattered. If it wasn't for her, I don't know where I would be. People will always be my biggest kryptonite, but she was the only one who didn't make me feel like an alien.

Snapping me out of my thoughts, Lila told me, "Don't worry about your book. There's no shame in taking a little bit of time to yourself. Don't give up, okay? For now, put it on the back burner, and just see what life has in store for you."

"Thanks. I mean it. I appreciate it." I forced a smile and nodded.

I did. I was hugely grateful. I just had no idea how to do any of that. What could possibly be enough to distract me from my colossal failure?

"Uh oh. Spoiled rich girl at twelve o'clock. I'm outta here."

Oh, fun. Elle Gonzales.

Lila and I exchanged brief head nods before parting ways. I assume she went out the front door, but I ducked beneath the checkout counter, letting Olive, my aloof coworker, handle the incoming chaos. Attempting to be inconspicuous, I grabbed some cleaning wipes and awkwardly scrubbed the bottom of my office chair. It was dusty anyway.

Olive flatly greeted her, "Your dad should be wrapping up his latest tour now. You can leave his lunch at his desk if you want."

"Cool, thanks." I heard Elle's flip-flops smack the floor of the lobby. When the noise got fainter, I knew the coast was clear.

As soon as I got up, I flinched when I saw a bright turquoise and pink floral print blouse. I lifted my eyes anyway, seeing the middle-aged blonde woman who worked as our assistant manager.

"Way to show initiative, Jenny! I thought it looked a little dusty down there. Good eye!" Amelia chirped.

"Aha...thanks..." I tried playing it cool.

"She was hiding from Elle again," Olive chimed in, the snitch.

Amelia sighed and shook her head, disappointed but not surprised, "I see. Well, at least you're keeping busy. In the future though, you may want to work on your people skills to save you some awkwardness."

Easier said than done.

"Come on, we better get going to the conference room. Mr. Gonzales said after the tour that he had a lot he wanted to talk about. Olive, hold down the fort while we're gone!" Amelia went over to her work station, collecting her things before heading for the staircase.

I stayed close, trying to catch up as we headed upstairs. When I looked back, Olive had already slid her some bulky headphones over her ears. I bit back a smirk and continued trailing behind Amelia until we reached the Carlyle room—one of the many old hotel rooms now serving as a conference room.

The bookstore went through so many different owners and investors, I wasn't sure which one finally won in the fight against the city for this building. They wanted to make it either a museum to the town's history or a bookstore, so this was the compromise. They restored the vintage decor and authentic artifacts, then threw in some bookshelves with sale signs on them.

I loved this room. It looked like a place where an old 1930's detective would tell a dinner party that the murderer was amongst them. It was classic and spooky—two traits that happen to be prevalent in my own aesthetic as well.

Once the tour ended, Mr. Gonzales joined us and opened the staff meeting. "Alright, people. We've been operating steadily this summer, but we're starting to lose traction. Last year, we had the benefit of being the shiny new attraction in town, but we need new ideas before the public gets bored of us."

He went around the table, putting paper down that each of us could use to take notes. At the top was today's date and each of the staff's names so we could keep track of attendance. Timothy Gonzales, building director, check. Amelia Snow, assistant regional manager, check. Jenevieve Weston, sales clerk (me), check. Andy Smith, IT and media specialist, check. Olive King, sales clerk, exempt for work. James Shepherd, security guard, exempt for work. Linda Crabtree, sales clerk...not checked. Maybe she was running behind today.

"Do we need more ideas already? We've practically just gotten started..." Amelia gave a nervous laugh.

Gonzales kept going as if he didn't hear her concern, "I was thinking of some sort of event or a program. Especially something geared toward young adults. We've got kids coming in regularly and our elderly patrons are always interested in history, but that middle ground is tricky. The only thing that seems to grab people these days are the tours. The haunted one, especially. I had a couple people come here from Michigan because they heard this place was haunted."

I saw out of the corner of my eye that Amelia and Andy had exchanged wary looks. The former spoke up first, "Mr. Gonzales, are you sure it's the best way to represent the town? After all, who knows where Beaumont's descendants are? They may be offended by this portrayal of their family's legacy. The magician was honored for his career, it may be considered offensive to glamorize his death."

"Honestly? With the rumors of his helping people smuggle alcohol during Prohibition, a ghost story isn't the worst way to represent him," Andy wryly said under his breath.

Amelia kept going once she got started, "Not to mention the kids! They might take things too far, like with social media. They come in here playing like ghost hunters or they try to skateboard in the lobby, ugh."

Suddenly, a welcome distraction rushed through the door just in time, "Sorry I'm late!"

Our only missing member of the meeting, Linda Crabtree, the oldest employee of Wax & Ink. A short woman with square glasses and graying hair she had kept up in a clip. Secretly, she was my favorite person to work with but I think she was everybody's favorite, due to her warm smile and constant energy that belonged to someone half her age.

"Sorry, everybody. I tripped coming up the stairs. Jimmy had to help me, the poor boy. Just a little tumble, but he insisted on making sure I was alright."

I rested my cheek in my hand and fought back a grin. Of course he did.

"Aw, Linda! Please be more careful or you're going to worry all of us." Amelia whined and shook her head.

"Mr. Gonzales, could you please catch me up on what I missed?" Linda tried hard to change the subject with an urging wave of her hand.

"We were brainstorming on programs or event ideas to help keep our numbers steady. Especially focusing on the young adult demographic." Gonzales began, happy to pick up where he left off.

As he went into his thoughts all over again, I saw some conversation was still going on the side, much to Linda's chagrin. Andy had murmured to her, "There's no shame in taking the elevator, Linda."

The elderly woman just waved her hand again, sharper this time as if she were swatting away an annoying fly. Meanwhile, I was thinking about more ideas for programs.

What were book-related things that people did for fun?

"Have you thought about doing a book club or something?" I suggested, "Do you think that's a good idea? Something lighthearted, kind of classic?"

Gonzales thought for a moment then hummed approvingly, "I don't see why we can't do that. We have rooms to use. That's an idea. Who would we get to organize something like this? Anyone here have the time?"

We all had the same idea and looked at Amelia, our reliable social butterfly, but to my disappointment, she was shaking her head, "Oh, that normally sounds like something I'd love to do but I'm way too behind on making up the schedule for next month."

"Well, I can't do it. I've got the tours. Does anyone here have any time on their hands for a new project?"

Project.

My mind echoed when Lila used that very word. She had suggested something just like this at work to get my mind off my book. Thinking about carrying this out made me feel queasy, though. I shouldn't have mentioned the book club idea at all. I'd never organized anything like this before. That sounded like a lot of socializing. Yeah, I had the time and it would give me something to do, but–

"I, uh, I don't have anything going on right now." Did I just say that?

Linda gasped, "Aw, that would be perfect. You'd do so good at that!"

I would?

"Yeah, and you're young. Like, 19, right? You're right in that age demographic we're looking for," Amelia agreed, "You can even pick the genre you want to theme the club after. You'd probably bring a lot of kids in."

Everyone seemed to have a misguided idea of what my social life looked like. I was a people-pleaser, sure, but what part of my personality said that I would enjoy something like this? I had Lila, but she was the only real friend I needed. I just had to keep reminding myself this was for the project. *Just the project.* I was sure I could manage that.

Until Gonzales chimed in, "Hey, I can invite my daughter to it too! You're about the same age. There you go, Miss Jenevieve, that can be your first book club member."

Under the table, my knee bounced up and down, getting faster with every idea my coworkers had to contribute. As if the idea of being in a room full of strangers wasn't inducing enough panic, now I had to worry about Elle coming? What could she possibly contribute? The only stuff I've seen her read were fashion magazines and social media posts.

"Are you sure you're up for this though, Jenevieve? We don't want to put any pressure on you." Andy seemed to be the only one who noticed my discomfort.

Everyone else in the room eyed me with anticipation. I slapped my hand on my knee to stop it from bouncing when I said, "I guess it wouldn't hurt to try."

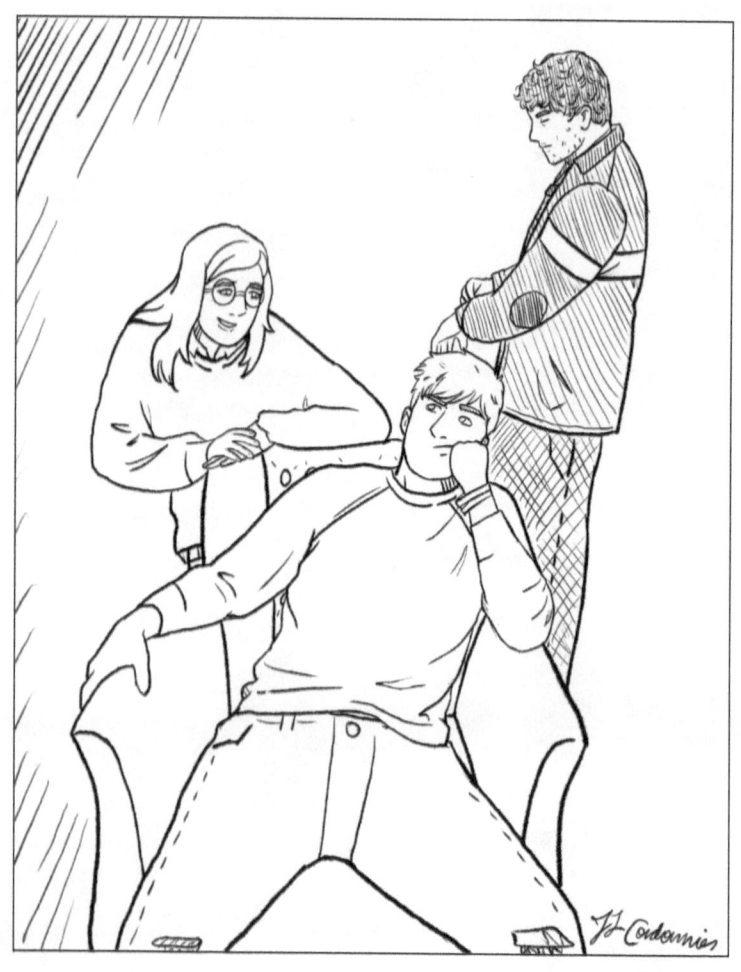

CHAPTER 2
RECRUITMENT

My knuckles were white as I gripped the railing, headed downstairs, and tried to gather my thoughts. A lot went into making a book club. I had to reserve the Carlyle room in advance, get decorations, maybe arrange for food to be catered for the first meeting, and all while staying under budget. All of that is fine. That could even be fun.

I was tasked with choosing a theme. Mystery was my favorite, that was a no-brainer, but then I'd have to navigate an hour-long conversation with multiple people. What would I say? How would I keep their attention? Leave it to me to take an idea as simple and stereotypically relaxing as a book club, and turn it into a big problem.

I quickly found that suffering through small talk was only the beginning. When I reached the bottom of the staircase, I saw my cousin standing with the building's security guard. Predictably, my eyes fell on James first–the way his coffee-colored locks fell over his brow. My heart fluttered. Hearing Memphis' snarky tone snapped me out of it, forcing my attention back on him.

"This is stupid. I hope you realize that." My cousin complained.

"You think I want to be here with you all the time?" James retorted.

"What did you do now?" My question must have come out louder than I meant it to because both of them immediately looked at me.

"I didn't do anything–I've been trying to tell him!" He motioned accusingly towards the man with the badge.

James looked around, concerned that we'd be disturbing other patrons. He let out a sigh and lowered his voice, "An employee found him in the bathroom upstairs. He and his friends were passing a, uh, smoke around."

"Just like...a regular cigarette, right?" I hoped.

He gave me a look.

"Oh my gosh. Memphis!"

"Okay, first off, I didn't do any smoking–and even if I did, it's not illegal."

The severity of the situation, as always, escaped him. Predictability was a family trait, I guess.

"You still have to be 21, and there's no smoking inside the store," James folded his arms and leveled his gaze at him, "Try again."

"If you weren't smoking, you should've left the room, Memphis..." I felt like his mother. I wonder how she'd feel if she knew her son would fall into patterns like this. On second thought, it wouldn't matter—if she didn't care to stick around, she wouldn't care where her kid ended up. "You ever hear the saying, 'Would you jump off a bridge if your friends did it too?'"

Memphis held a finger to his lips and hummed, feigning thoughtfulness as if he were considering his answer. He took a second or two and then he said, "Maybe if I had a bungee cord attached to it...now that would be kind of fun."

He was incorrigible. I growled and threw my hands up in defeat, but James looked away and took a breath until the tension in his jaw released.

Memphis only shrugged. He walked with us into the lobby where he promptly threw himself into one of the leather wingback chairs in front of the fireplace. I eyed him for a few seconds to make sure he stayed still before I turned around. I folded my arms and paced over the maroon oriental rug. For a moment, I glanced over at James but the instant he looked back and our eyes met, mine darted right back to that carpet.

I couldn't believe Memphis had embarrassed me again. He couldn't have gotten in trouble at school? He had to bring it to my place of work? *In front of James?* I didn't want him to think my family was nuts. I mean, we were, but I didn't want to scare him off.

Something about the sleepy security guard reminded me of sinking into an old leather chair. A little worn, but comfy and made you feel safe. He was humble and didn't call attention to himself, but he had a slightly husky, deeper voice that made you want to lean in and listen. A scruffy beard littered his square jaw and I was obsessed with his messy curls. He was handsomely masculine but in an underrated, down-to-earth sort of way.

When I had finally gathered some strength to talk to him, I made my way over, "I'm sorry about Memphis. Thanks for dealing with him without calling too much attention to it."

"Don't mention it."

"I just don't know what's gotten into him. He used to be such a good kid, and now it's something freshly problematic every day.." I shook my head in disbelief.

While some of us tried to grow up and become responsible, he was actively fighting against adulthood. Some kids made fun of his dad, so he felt it was appropriate to deck them in the face. Then he cheated on a test by printing the answers out on a water bottle label. Then there was the time he and his friends raced dirt bikes in the school parking lot after-hours...

Yet, everything remained a joke to him. This was only mildly concerning when he was 16, but now he was a senior. If he didn't shape up this year, what was he going to do after he graduated? When he didn't have his dad to save him all the time.

It was all the more concerning what he was getting into, what this could be the beginning of. We had a bit of a drug problem in Waxwood. Despite being such a small town, comfortable middle class majority, I could still hear the firetruck's sirens before noon every day. Not because of fires, but because an addict had overdosed. I didn't want to see the day my cousin was one of those unfortunate people. I dreaded where he may end up if he didn't get himself together now.

As James and I talked, he merely shrugged. One of the few frustrating things about him—he was a man of few words.

I looked back at Memphis, remembering, yet again, Lila's advice on finding a new hobby. That could very well apply to him too. Maybe if I invited him, he could come around and we'd get to see each other more, like we did when we were kids.

Optimistic, I folded my arms over the back of the wingback chair beside him. "You need a better pastime."

"Look, I don't want another lecture, okay?" Memphis eyed me warily.

"I'm not here to lecture," I held my hands up in surrender, "But maybe you could try your hand at something more relaxing...like reading?"

"You read and you're the most stressed-out person I've ever met."

Touche, cuz, touche.

The resemblance between us was strong. When we were kids on the playground, some people mistook us for siblings. We both had dark blonde hair, and hazel eyes that were brown from a distance, but green up close. The main difference these days was our skin tones. I was deathly pale while he was tanned–showing who spent more time outdoors and who hid in her room and read.

"Listen, I'm starting a book club for work. It would mean a lot to me if you could be there. You're one of the few people I'm comfortable around and it would make things a lot less awkward for me."

He exhaled, avoiding eye contact. Even though he was reclining lazily in the seat, Memphis's knee was bobbing violently like he was waiting to pop, "Books aren't my thing."

Nothing I didn't already assume. But I was desperate. He needed less sketchy activities and better friends. Plus, I didn't want to be stuck in a room with a bunch of strangers and...Elle. This could work out for us both if he gave me the chance.

I walked around the chair and then sat down in the seat beside him. I needed a different approach. I chewed my lip and turned my eyes down, lowering my shoulders as if I were hurt,

"You just don't want to spend time with me like you used to."

Memphis furrowed his eyebrows, "That's not what I said. That's not..."

"It's what you mean though. Is it because I'm boring? Because I like different stuff than you?"

"Jenevieve," Memphis started to sit up, leaning in with more interest for the conversation, "Don't talk like that. I still like to spend time with you. You're not boring. It's–"

I playfully narrowed my eyes at him and pursed my lips, "I see. You think you're too cool for book club."

Realizing now he was set up, he started to laugh, "Stop. That's not what I said."

"'Oh I'm Memphis. I play basketball. I'm cool. I don't read. I'm like Kareem Abdul-Jabbar. Because he certainly has never read before." I mocked. I was resorting to less-than-mature means, but like I said, I was desperate.

Knowing I wasn't the sports type, he instantly gave me an incredulous look, "You know who Kareem Abdul-Jabbar is?"

"Because I read!"

It was the truth. I learned who that basketball player was because I found out in a non-canon Sherlock Holmes book that he was a huge fan of the famous character too.

Memphis just scoffed and shook his head, "Is there going to be any food at this thing?"

I grinned, "I could arrange that."

"We'll see."

I could take that. *"We'll see,"* is better than *"No."* It wasn't so painful inviting someone to join a book club after all.

Maybe I could even invite James...

I glanced up at his frame as he stood by the window, waiting for my uncle. His hands were shoved into his pockets and the sun shone on his brown eyes. I couldn't quite tell from where I stood, but I wondered if they looked gold in the light or if they had green flecks in them...

I snapped out of my reverie with a wince. I couldn't invite him to the book club. Him and Memphis in the same room? Probably not a good idea. Besides, it's not like I'd ever have the nerve to ask.

A police car soon pulled up to the front of the building and a tall man with graying hair, a goatee, and a uniform came inside. Through the doors, I could see him tighten his jaw before entering. He looked at James and shook his hand.

"Hey, thanks for holding him for me. I'm sorry you had to babysit. Again."

"It's no problem, sir," James nodded respectfully.

"Nobody has to babysit me." Memphis said through gritted teeth, folding his arms and leaning back in the chair as his dad drew closer, "I'm basically an adult."

"If you were an adult, you would be getting trespassed from this building and getting threatened with a jail cell." Uncle Wyatt rested his hands on his belt as he stood over him, "We wouldn't have to go through this rigmarole if you'd shape up and quit your nonsense."

"I didn't even do anything!" Memphis jerked up from his chair and motioned emphatically.

James and I exchanged awkward looks. Just when everything had started to cool down..

"Your behavior today says otherwise, kid!" After he snapped, Uncle Wyatt looked around self-consciously, as if remembering where he was. He exhaled sharply then cleared his throat, "We'll talk about this in the car. Come on."

My uncle took Memphis by the hood of his sweatshirt like a lion would hold his cub by the scruff of their neck. On their way out, I could still hear their bickering in hushed tones, unable to contain themselves till the car.

Uncle Wyatt wryly called back from over his shoulder, "Have a good one!" Just before they went out the door.

"Wow, a book club." My dad let out a whistle after I had relayed the day's events. "How do we feel about that?

I kept my head down, my fork pushing around a piece of broccoli that had probably gone cold, "Well, Lila was proud of me for getting myself out there. Something to distract myself from the, uh, whole rejection thing. Maybe get out there. Socialize some."

"Exciting!" my mom grinned.

"But Elle's dad said he was going to invite her." I cringed, "So she might come and be...who she is. Or I could just fail at making a good book club."

"Ooh, not exciting," Dad joked before sobering again. "I know you're going to anyway, but try not to stress about all of this. There are so many what-ifs that could happen. All you can do is pray about it, give it your best shot, and let God handle everything else."

"Excellent advice, Joseph," Mom praised.

"Why thank you."

"I hope Memphis comes too," she continued, "I worry about him a lot. Wyatt needs to be spending more time with him."

"That's not any of our business, Faye…"

Mom merely huffed at Dad's warning.

I forced the lukewarm broccoli into my mouth, my mind wandering to everything I'd need to get done the next day. Probably go to the craft store and get some decorations. Hopefully, they had some pieces that could pass for the theme—like some fake blood or police tape. Handcuffs could work as a centerpiece. When I was starting to feel more optimistic, I shook my head, silently dashing my own hopes. Life wasn't like a book. In a story, you know where everything is going and that whatever happens has a purpose. Real life was so much messier.

"What's wrong, baby? You've been quiet," Mom wrinkled her brow in concern.

"I just wish Mint had accepted my book. Or any book I've written."

"Well, he has some nerve to reject my girl." Mom got up from the dinner table when she finished her food then went to the sink, roughly spraying her plate off with the hose. "She's been writing since the third grade. Don't tell me my baby can't write! She has a gift!"

"No one said she couldn't write. Calm down. This isn't personal." Dad got up next, taking his plate and setting it down in the sink, not even blinking when my mom gave him the stink eye. Over what he said or by adding another plate to her dish work, I wasn't sure which.

"He wasn't being mean, Mom. The guy just said it wasn't what they're looking for." I sat back in my chair, giving up on my plate. Even if I knew it would just make for sad leftovers the next day.

"See? She's not freaking out so we don't need to be," Dad tried again to placate her.

Mom nodded in understanding and then started to calm down. It looked like his attempts had finally worked. It was silent in the dining area for 8 seconds before I made the mistake of murmuring,

"You think this is God's sign He doesn't want me to be a writer?"

"Oh, here we go!" Dad threw back his head with a groan, "Don't you start. We've been over this."

"God wouldn't have given you this gift for no reason, Jenevieve! This guy is just a stupid head." Mom's face scrunched up in her anger and she gave a definitive nod, confident in her assessment, even as dad mouthed the words and squinted at the ceiling, incredulous. "If this publisher couldn't tell you were talented from the short stories you've already published, then he just can't do his job. There are other publishers out there. Plenty of famous authors have been rejected before too. Tell her, Joseph, she won't listen to me."

"Well, Dr. Seuss didn't–"

She didn't let him finish his thought. Or even begin his thought.

"Mary Higgins Clark didn't start publishing mysteries until she was fifty-one, I think."

"Faye Elaine! Don't ask for help then interrupt me..." Dad gave an exasperated laugh.

To which, she just giggled, "Heh, sorry."

He sighed then started again, "Forget other writers. The point is, rejection is not a '*not ever.*' It is just a '*not now.*' Besides, this isn't your career right now. You still live with us and you have the bookstore. You're only nineteen years old. You have time to figure out what story is your life's work. It may just take a little more experience."

I smiled weakly, "I just hope that will come soon."

CHAPTER 3
A SIMPLE BOOK CLUB

I was numb all day.

It didn't hit me when Mom took a picture of my outfit, or when I was picking up the decorations from the store. It didn't hit me when I walked through the door of the bookshop. When I went into the Carlyle room—there it hit me. It wasn't even nerves, exactly. There weren't any butterflies or nausea. I just remember walking into that empty room and feeling like this was the beginning of something. A shift in the atmosphere. Things were changing. I just had to pray it was for the better.

"Thanks again for your help decorating, Lila," I said, an hour later. "I know this feels excessive, but I want to make this as memorable as possible."

"Oh, this is memorable for me already." She joked as she was lying on the floor in an exaggerated fallen pose so I could maneuver white tape around her body like the police would at a crime scene.

"I hope the tape and the table don't clash…"

Once Lila was on her feet again, I analyzed the work surface I had adorned with a lace table runner, the books I'd stacked in the middle with my Holmes hat on top and the candelabras I had put on either side of the centerpiece. It looked authentic, if I dared say so myself. The old-fashioned, spooky room had finally lived up to its potential.

"I want it to look like a fancy dinner party turned into a crime scene—like something out of an Agatha Christie novel."

Lila smoothed down her denim overall dress, "Trust me, you got it. Everything looks perfect."

"Thanks," I sighed in relief. "Now I just need to put the police tape on the window."

I reached for the bright yellow tape I had set on one of the chairs, but before I could grab it, I saw someone had come to the door. Thankfully, it was just Linda and Andy, carrying boxes. Once I got a good whiff, I could tell what goodies there were inside.

"The catering service just dropped off the food! Make sure to thank Andy. Isn't he a gentleman?" Linda looked about ready to pinch his cheek.

"Ah, it's no big deal," Andy blushed a little as he readjusted his grip on the big box. "Where do you want 'em?"

"Oh, just over here against the wall would be fine," I gestured. "I want a buffet-style side table separate from the meeting table, so people can grab what they want. Thanks so much." I stepped out of his way and put my hands together, excited to see how my order turned out.

"Hey, the lid's been opened. Did you sneak a bite?" Lila eyed him.

"Maybe..." Andy gave a cheeky little wink.

I laughed, "It'll be his payment, it's fine. How does it look though?"

"Red velvet cupcakes with tiny knives stabbed into them. Cute." Lila shot me a thumbs-up.

I hurried to set out everything and view all of the results with pride. It was a nice, diverse spread. We had finger sandwiches, potato chips, soda, fruit punch, and those cupcakes. On the healthier side, we had a veggie platter of cold broccoli, cauliflower, and carrots with a small saucer of ranch dressing in the center.

"Are you sure you have enough food?" Andy joked.

"Oh, hush. This is her first book club. Everything looks really good, Jen." Linda paused and looked me up and down, "You look so pretty too, but, uh, isn't it a bit warm indoors for a trench coat?"

I looked down at my outfit. After two days of debating what to wear, I finally chose a black turtleneck with a set of pearls over it, blue jeans, black chunky loafers with a gold chain over the top, a black headband, and a trench coat over it all.

"It's classic detective fashion," I was quick to reply "The sacrifice was required and we have an oscillating fan, it's fine."

"If you insist." Linda chuckled.

"Thanks again for agreeing to cover my shift tonight. Are you and Olive going to be okay?" I perused the table, carefully adjusting the deerstalker so it sat perfectly on top of its book podium.

"Olive left early. She's going home sick." Andy spoke up.

"Oh shoot. You're going to be here, though, right, Andy?"

"My shift ended 15 minutes ago, man."

"Stop worrying about me! I'm a big girl. I can handle a little shift by myself," Linda contended, with her hands on her hips.

"Okay, okay. I'm sorry," I held my hands up. "Thank you both for all your help, though. You too, Lila!"

She was too distracted making herself a plate at the snack table to reply with more than a vague, "Uh-huh, sure..."

"Well, we'll leave you kids to it. Good luck!" Linda gave us a little wave before walking out with Andy.

Just as quickly as our first visitors left, a new set arrived. If I had had five guesses, I wouldn't have predicted who would walk into my book club. If I had seen his escort first, I probably would've predicted it in three.

Uncle Wyatt was in full police captain uniform and badge. Based on the firm grip he had on Memphis' shoulder, I didn't think cuz had much of a choice.

"Hey, Jenny. Hope you don't mind that we came. I don't want him lollygagging around, so I figured a book club would be the last place he'd get into trouble."

"Sure, I don't mind at all," I chirped.

"Thanks. You kids have fun!" Wyatt pointed at Memphis before he left, "You better behave, alright? Read a book or something, maybe you'll get smarter."

"Yeah, yeah. Whatever. I don't need—are those red velvet?" Memphis' sour expression immediately dissolved as soon as he saw the snack table. He wasn't kidding when he said he'd need to be bribed with food. That was surprisingly easy.

"Yep. This is exactly how I pictured this." A new but not unfamiliar voice quickly put me on edge. I knew before I turned around that Elle had shown up, like I feared she would.

And you're just how I remember you. I bit my tongue before I could say that out loud. If we were going to get through this, I'd have to leave the past behind and try to be civil. She was starting strong tonight with a backhanded comment. She hadn't changed much at all from when we were kids. Except now, she made an oversized gray sports team sweatshirt, black bicycle shorts, and sandals look...expensive. How did she do that?

Elle's dark hair was slicked back into a clip, two thin strands of her bangs left out purposely so they framed her face beautifully. I'm sure any guy she meets would assume her look is effortlessly perfect.

Apparently, except for Memphis. Out of the corner of my eye, I caught him giving her a double-take, followed by a dirty look.

"Hey, Elle," I forced a smile. "Thanks for coming."

"Thank my dad." She slid her purse off her shoulder and then lowered herself into one of the chairs at the table.

Lila and I exchanged knowing looks. Though Lila didn't go to school with us growing up, she likely remembered Elle as the girl who ratted us out to my uncle when we were twelve.

"Well, gee, if I had known a princess was coming to join us then I would've dressed up more." Memphis walked over and set his plate down at his spot. He sat down and rested his face in his hand, giving her a mocking little nose scrunch. There was a good chance he remembered her too.

Elle didn't answer his question, but rather cocked her brow and snarled her upper lip. This wasn't going in the direction I had planned.

I went to my spot and picked up a list. I had scoured the internet for book club prompts to use, hoping to keep the group flowing and to keep myself from getting lost.

My eyes landed on the top of the list. "Alright! Why don't we go around and, aha, introduce ourselves?"

It was an unavoidable tradition for gatherings like these. *Oh* no, did everyone know each other? Was no one else coming in? I looked down the list but it didn't make sense unless I went in order. Well, maybe not everyone remembers each other from that little awkward introduction when we were kids. This was our chance to start fresh.

"I'm Jenevieve Weston, but you can call me Jen since it's shorter. I'm a salesclerk here at Wax & Ink. I'm a big reader, with Sherlock being my favorite to...you know, read. I'm nineteen years old and I like antiques, writing, drawing, and, uh, playing the piano."

I reached for a cup of punch and took a big gulp to soothe my suddenly dry throat. Thank God that was over.

My dear, old reliable best friend picked up the ball and went next, "Uh, I'm Lila Greene. I met Jen when we were around 10 when my family moved here from Michigan. We met at church and we've been two peas in a pod ever since. I'm in my second year in nursing school. I collect cool rocks, mushrooms, cozy socks, and I love mixing toxic chemicals together."

"Lovely. Thank you, Lila. Who would like to go next?" I looked at Elle and Memphis.

"Well, I–" Elle began but she got cut off.

"Hi. I'm Memphis," his tone was surprisingly serious, "And I've been an alcoholic for ten years now."

Lila snorted at his joke then mockingly waved to him, "Hi, Memphis."

I blinked at him, my lips pursed into a thin line to keep from smiling. Okay, I should've seen that coming. I just let that one go. Memphis needs little introduction at this point. I turned to Elle, who was now glaring at Memphis.

"Uh, I'm Elle. I knew Jen back in school. I'm not big on reading, but I like volleyball, self-care, and iced coffee. I'm studying cosmetology so I can be, like, a professional makeup artist or something like that."

"How unique of you," Memphis mocked, just making her glare at him worse.

I sucked in my lips. As entertaining as this was, I took my pen and scratched off the top question before going to the next step, "Okay! Now that we're all good and introduced, let me just pass this around. You can pay for them after the club's over if you're interested in coming back for more meetings."

I brought out the wooden cart carrying stacks of the book I decided we'd read. Matching red books with Sherlock's profile silhouette on the cover. A Study in Scarlet. Once everyone had their copies, Elle raised a brow with hesitation while Memphis opened up the book and just started skimming the pages. When he started to lose the color in his face, it occurred to me that not everyone might appreciate the Victorian terminology. At least Lila was grinning supportively.

I looked at my list again. I think the nerves were getting to me. I readjusted my glasses until the lines were aligned together again. I blinked once or twice, then smiled when I saw we had reached the part I knew by heart.

"'This is the first Sherlock story written by Sir Arthur Conan Doyle. He had two main inspirations for his character. The first was Edgar Allan Poe's C. Auguste Dupin, and the second was Doyle's real-life mentor, Joseph Bell. Both men had a unique ability to be able to read people just based on what they saw on their person.'"

"I love that there was a real-life Sherlock." My emotional support friend was at it again. "Didn't you once tell me he helped police on cases too?"

"He did!" I nodded eagerly. "He helped with the Jack the Ripper case. He wrote in a letter who he thought did it at the end, but they never publicly released what he wrote."

"Was that the case where the British dude killed off all those—" Memphis began with a little smirk but Elle cut him off.

"Unfortunate women? Yeah. That's what she's talking about," Elle shuddered. "It's hard enough trying to live in a world dominated by men but then you have to resort to such a dangerous job trying to make ends meet. Then just when you think your life can't get any worse, this guy slaughters them like nothing!"

She held a perfectly manicured hand to her heart and took a slow sip of her punch. Memphis shot her a look, his lips pursed from the frustration of being interrupted. He looked down and furrowed his brows before blinking a couple times. Did she make him speechless? That was a first.

"Right! It's awful. That's why there needs to be detectives." I held up the book, continuing our introduction to the Sherlock Holmes novels. So far, this hasn't been going too badly. We had a couple hiccups, and I wasn't sure how natural the flow felt to everyone, but we looked like we were on the brink of connecting over my favorite genre.

That was until we heard a scream.

Elle flinched, nearly spilling her drink "What was that?!"

Lila slowly turned to me. "I don't remember that being part of the ambiance plans when we were decorating."

"That's because I, uh, didn't plan that."

"Sounds like we need to check it out." Memphis was all too ready to hop out of his chair. I almost suspected he might've schemed some way to get out of here, but I quickly dismissed the notion.

"No, no! I can call Linda downstairs and ask what's going on. You guys stay here where it's safe and I will–" Before I finished my sentence, Elle and Memphis were already out the door. I blinked in disbelief, "Did I even say anything?"

Lila got up next. "Come on. Someone might get hurt. We might as well all go." It was becoming apparent I didn't have a choice in our plan of action. The book club tips online didn't prepare me for this.

Memphis led the way down the hall, adding over his shoulder, "Horror movie rules, Jen. No splitting up."

I was, admittedly, grateful for their stubbornness. I didn't know what was going on and I certainly didn't want to be alone if there was trouble. I wanted to be competent in my job and make my guests feel safe, but I was getting the growing feeling something was horribly wrong.

That was when we found Linda..

Blood gushed from her head onto the vintage rug in a way that made the floor sway beneath me. I heard a gasp. I assumed it was Elle, but maybe I had gasped too. I don't remember. I couldn't believe it. She was my sweet elderly coworker. The one who pinched cheeks and praised everyone. The one who had a date every other weekend. The one who worked with twice the energy I had was now sprawled lifeless at the bottom of the staircase.

A wave of nausea went through me and I didn't know if I was going to faint or throw up. My face felt so hot and the world around me was sloshing like water in a rubber bottle.

"Hey, you!" Memphis pointed back up the staircase.

I don't know what he was pointing out, exactly. I could have sworn I saw a white blob of some kind. A colorless blur, suddenly moving hurriedly in the opposite direction down the hall where we couldn't see. Memphis took off up the stairs after it, like a bullet out of a gun.

"Memphis, don't!" I heard myself cry out.

Just like before, he didn't listen to me. I heard his sneakers squeak on the wooden steps where he awkwardly swerved but he kept on racing. So much for not splitting up. As much as I wanted to know who that was, I prayed Memphis didn't find them. Because whoever it was, they were the reason Linda was now on the floor.

"Oh my gosh! Oh my gosh! What do we do??" Elle held her hands to her heart, her breath getting shallower, working herself into hyperventilation, "Is there a doctor?"

Doctor? I held a hand to my temple as I tried to gather my scattered thoughts. *Doctor...doctor...*it was like the word was making my brain itch. Oh yeah! I looked at Lila, "You're kinda trained. Can you do something? Can you help her? Please?!"

"Oh, me!" Lila's brows flew up, waking up from the shock. She hurried to Linda and gently shook her first, "Linda, Linda. Can you hear me? Are you ok?"

"Obviously she's not okay! She's got blood coming out of her head!" Elle snapped.

"It's the order you're supposed to do things!" Lila shot back. "Call 911! Jen, I-I need a first aid kit and an AED!" She lowered herself close to Linda's mouth, trying to listen to her breathing.

AED, what was that again? Right, the white box with the heart with the lightning bolt on it. I nodded eagerly and hurried to get what Lila needed while she took off her olive jacket and wrapped it around Linda's head, trying to stop the bleeding. Elle took out her phone and shakily dialed the number.

"Pl-please come help us! We're at Wax & Ink and a woman just fell down the stairs! We need help!" I heard Elle's cries echoing in the lobby as I reached the security room.

My heart stopped when I saw James. His arms were folded over his desk. He was slumped over, completely still. After seeing what happened to Linda, I thought something had happened to him too. I went to check his pulse and thank the Lord, he was alive. But when I heard soft snoring, all my worry turned into anger. Did he seriously fall asleep on the job? Of all the times to do that, this was the day he chose to slack off.

"Wake up! Wake up! Linda's hurt–wake up!" I grabbed his arm and shook him.

He groaned when he began to stir. He slowly lifted his head and looked at me with drooping eyes, threatening to close again at any moment, "What's...what's happening? What's wrong?" His words slurred together.

"Linda needs help! Now! Where have you been?! She's hurt!" I snapped at him, staring at him in disbelief. This moment had put a crack in the lens of my rose-colored glasses.

"Forget it! I gotta get the first aid kit and the IE–ADD– the thing!!" I stumbled over my words, trying to fight my way through the panic threatening to overtake me. I snatched the AED and first aid kit from their container in the wall then I rushed out of the room, not caring to check back to see if he was following me or not. I just wanted to focus on Linda. On getting her the help she needed. Before it was too late.

"Don't panic! I got the first aid kit!" I slid back to my knees. I opened the plastic white kit and set it between Lila and myself, "What do you need? Can I get anything?"

"I just need this!" Lila scrambled for the AED, opening it up and pressing a button to turn it on, "Can you cut through her shirt for me? I need to get these patches on her torso."

"Oh my gosh..." Elle wept into her hand, her mascara running down her cheeks.

"Okay, okay!" I took the scissors in the kit then cut through Linda's shirt. Once it was open, Lila placed one patch on her chest and the other between her lower torso and her side. Lila's hands were shaking like a leaf.

"Stay clear of patient. Analyzing," a robotic woman's voice said from the machine. *"Shock advised. Stay clear of patient."*

"Guys, back up, no one touch her!" Lila waved her arms for Elle and I to step back just as the machine announced, *"Delivering electric shock."* There was a short pause, and then, *"Shock delivered. Begin CPR."*

Lila started pressing on her chest, counting under her breath.

I watched, frozen in shock. I could hear my pounding heart thudding in my eardrums. I prayed in my head that Linda survive this. *Please, God, don't let her die. Don't let her die...*

"The guy on the phone says be calm—everyone, be calm!" Elle told us, but I'm pretty sure no one was calm. Lila may have been the closest. Out of the three of us, she was the only one not in shock. That nurse training looked to be paying off, and if I felt any slight comfort in this situation, it helped to know somebody knew what they were doing.

"What happened?!" James staggered into the room, his eyes widening when his gaze landed on our fallen colleague. He swayed for a moment, then ran a hand down his face. His forehead had already broken out with perspiration. No one answered his question.

"Stay clear of patient. Analyzing," the machine continued *"Stay clear of patient. Analyzing...analyzing..."*

CHAPTER 4
THE AFTERMATH

Make a book club, they said. *Meet new people, and talk about shared interests. Get more experience, then you'll have your story.* That's the essence of most of the advice I'd gotten. I don't think this is what any of them intended.

My ears were still ringing. Lila and I sat on the steps as the police worked around us. Some were looking around the whole building...or *perimeter,* I suppose they would call it. Forensic photographers took pictures of the scene while officers roped off the scene with yellow tape. Not a prop like in the Carlyle room, the real stuff.

On TV, it would look chaotic with everyone stepping over each other, but they moved with a surprising fluidity. No one tampered with the source of the scene, probably to protect any potential evidence.

I watched solemnly as the paramedics took Linda's body away. *Good grief. Her body.* I shuddered as I sat with a blanket the medics had given me wrapped around my shoulders. For shock or something, I didn't fully understand. *Shock* is such a simple word for the devastating mess we had all just experienced...

I'm sure Uncle Wyatt hadn't expected to come back so soon. Especially not to interview the club as witnesses. His personal life and his work life just collided. My uncle had just returned from his last interview. Apparently with Elle, because I could hear her complaining in the background about how no one would listen to her.

Off to the side, a paramedic was shining a light in James's eyes and calmly talking to him about what happened. Heh, what would he remember? He was asleep during most of it. For once, he was the last thing I wanted to think about. I didn't know what to make of his sleeping on the job yet. Was it just an honest mistake or...?

"Jenevieve?" My uncle called my name next.

I slowly rose from my place on the step, briefly mouthing my goodbyes to Lila, then followed him to the Carlyle room. I imagine he hoped to get me away from the crime scene and talk to me somewhere more private, but when he stepped into the room, I caught a glimpse of regret on Uncle Wyatt's face when he saw the crime scene decorations donning the walls and tables.

More police tape, fake blood, and even a white outline of a body on the floor. He cringed and took a sharp breath, but chose not to voice his mistake and just helped me get a seat at the table.

"Hey, how are you feeling?" His brows were knitted together in what I assumed was concern but he was careful to not carry over into the emotional or sympathetic realm. I guess that was the cop training in him.

"I don't know…" I admitted, clutching my blanket and rubbing the fabric between my fingers. I supposed, *numb*, would be the right word. It was like I was walking in a fog; my emotions couldn't catch up with the facts. I was aware of everything, but it was all too surreal. Like I was watching myself from an outsider's perspective, and all this was just an episode of another TV show.

Uncle Wyatt nodded in understanding before looking down at his notepad. Then his eyes shot up at me a second later. It was clear that it was time for the badge to come on. He was no longer my uncle, he was a police captain doing his duty.

"I know you've been through a lot tonight and that you likely just want to go home and rest. But we're gonna have to go through a few questions first, okay? Could you please describe the details of what happened?"

I complied, naturally, and summarized how the book club's first meeting played out until we heard the noise. I continued on with the details of how we followed that noise to find Linda Crabtree's body at the bottom of the stairs. I then finished with, "Memphis pointed out something and ran after it. Lila and James helped Linda the best they could, and Elle called for help."

"Did you see what Memphis saw?" I was surprised at the way he was able to remove emotion from his question. As if he was talking about a stranger and not his son.

"I'm not, uh, I'm not entirely sure. I saw a white blur. Like just a quick blur." *Yeah, super helpful, Jen. Wake up, stupid.* It didn't make sense, not even to me, but it was all I remembered, "I'm sorry. I didn't see much."

Uncle Wyatt didn't take notes until I had said that. Probably writing word for word, *'Jenevieve Weston says she didn't see much.'* That's the first thing that hit me funny.

"Did Memphis tell you what he saw?" I asked, "He probably saw it better than I did."

"Uh, let's focus on what *you* saw," the captain replied. "Is that all you can tell me about tonight?"

"I think so…" I picked at a loose thread on the blanket then looked up at him again, "I'm sorry I can't be more helpful. I don't know what to say."

"You told the truth and that's enough. Thank you for your time." He rose from the table and then held the door for me before we both took the elevator, purposely avoiding the staircase.

Once we made it to the main floor again, I saw Elle telling her father what had happened. Mr. Gonzales listened to her with wide eyes and his jaw slack like he had seen a ghost.

"Are you guys going to find out who did this?" I asked my uncle. "They could still be in this building."

He breathed out of his nose, "I assure you, we're being very thorough."

Over his shoulder, I saw a couple of his officers leaving the building. I forced my face to remain neutral. After they left, my parents barreled in. As soon as they saw me, I was engulfed in a group hug.

"My poor baby! I heard what happened! I heard the sirens and I just knew something was wrong! I could feel it! I'm so glad I prayed!" My mom smothered the side of my face in kisses. I was mad at James right now but I still hoped he didn't see this.

"She's a tough kid. I think she'll be just fine." The captain suddenly turned back into my uncle. He pinched my cheek for a second like I was twelve again, then with a reassuring wink, he went to the rest of the group for more interviews.

"I guess things didn't go to plan, huh?" Dad weakly joked.

"And then some," I exhaled.

"Don't worry, your uncle will handle everything. He does this for a living." My mom rubbed my back. "Go tell Lila to get her stuff. We'll take her home then we'll all get some rest."

As long as I can remember, I've always been a homebody. Even farther back than that. My parents still tell the story of when I was two years old, I would point out our house to them when they drove past it. I liked being at home in the comfort of my things, my way of living, but I didn't know what to do with myself now.

My dog Muffie rested on my belly while I mindlessly ran my fingers over her tufts of fur. She looked peaceful. Her eyes closed, and the way her whole body rose and fell with every breath. I, however, did not feel her peace. My heart was racing without actually beating harder than usual. A sense of impending doom, even though I was safe in bed. I tried to pray, but my every thought lingered to what had happened.

I could talk to Lila, but I knew she was in bed, trying to forget tonight, too. Then there was Memphis, Elle, and even James. What did you do after something like this happened? Normally, when I found the time, I would take out my laptop and get some writing in, but writing comes from the imagination, and mine was consumed with the question,

Who was that white figure that caused her blood to stain the carpet?

I never wanted this. Yes, I had wanted inspiration but not like this. I didn't even try to reel my mind back in. Aside from petting Muffie, I couldn't think of anything I could do to distract myself. So, I just gave into my head until I fell into a mercifully dreamless sleep.

CHAPTER 5
LINDA'S VIEWING

"I knew she'd get hurt on those steps one of these days! I knew it!" Amelia sniffed and tried to wipe away the tears on her cheeks.

Olive's eyes didn't leave the road as she reached for a box of tissues and handed them to Amelia, who sat beside her in the passenger seat. The bookstore was closed for the day so all of the staff could attend Linda's viewing. The family had requested that the funeral be family only, so this was our only chance to get to see her and pay our respects.

The whole experience made me sick the past couple of days. The day after, I just stayed in bed and cringed away from the sun. The numbness never left. How were you supposed to feel after witnessing a situation like that? I wasn't crying like Amelia, or hysterical like people in books.

It had taken a while to come out of the fog, but I had accepted it was real now. Linda truly wasn't here anymore. I still didn't know what to think. *What was it that Memphis saw that night? What did the police find after they searched the place? Was it an accident, or was there more to it?*

It just occurred to me that I hadn't talked to anyone in the club since the first meeting. I prayed in my head that they were doing alright, that they were stable. Were they numb like me? Were they traumatized? Was I traumatized? Was this what I was going through?

"Jen, you're bleeding..." Amelia's voice broke through my thoughts.

I looked down, seeing my fingernails were stained red from where I had been peeling away the skin on my lip.

"Oh."

"Here," Amelia shook her head and took out a couple more tissues before reaching over and handing them to me.

At the viewing, it was only more surreal when we passed Linda's casket. Although she was recognizable, it was evident they had to do something to her face. How did that process work anyway? She looked like a wax version of herself. It was hard to believe there used to be life in her breast, and now she was just gone. Why couldn't my book club have been on a different night? What if we had gotten there sooner? Could I have prevented what happened?

When I went to find a seat, I saw James was a few spaces behind me in line. He stayed at Linda's side for a while, longer than I noticed other people did. He rested his hands on the side of her casket, almost leaning against it, and shook his head. I wondered what he must be feeling. Guilt? It was still so hard to wrap my head around him falling asleep on the job the one night he was needed the most. Although, I suppose it was an innocent enough mistake. After all, nothing like this has happened before. If I had caught him on any other, boring day, I would have laughed it off. I guess it was just a matter of bad timing.

I felt bad enough that I wasn't at the desk with her when it happened. If I hadn't had book club that night, I would've been working with her. Then maybe she wouldn't have had to face whatever caused her fall. Sometimes I get so deep in my head replaying every scene, that I almost convince myself my rewrite was real for a second—but then I'll blink and it would be gone. The reality was yet another punch to the gut. And the process would start all over again.

"Psst! Jen! Jenny! Jenevieve! Cuz! Psst!"

I flinched when I heard my name before spinning around. I had to do a double-take when I saw my cousin a couple of pews behind me, sandwiched between Lila and Elle. What were they doing here? The only one that had a decent excuse to be here was likely Elle if she came with her dad, but why were they here as a group?

I furrowed my brows. "What are you guys doing here?"

"Gee, nice to see you too," Elle commented with a little smirk.

Memphis didn't answer my question, and instead asked one of his own, "Did they say what caused Linda's death yet?"

"Shh!" I warned, my eyes darting around to make sure no one else heard that. I'd be lucky if we didn't all get kicked out of the funeral home. What if the family had heard us?

Memphis didn't seem to understand my concerns. "What? Dad's been too busy to tell me."

"Is this really the place to talk about it? I don't even know what happened. No one's told me anything either."

Lila spoke up next. "Do you want to find out?"

I hesitated. My gaze drifted over to Amelia and Olive then to Linda's casket. The thought came back: *what if I had been able to do something to prevent her death?* We would have been there if we had just been seconds faster. I had so many questions. Who was it that Memphis chased out? Why did they run?

My curiosity conquered my hesitation and I chose to go with the others. I told Olive and Amelia I found another ride before following the club out to the parking lot, getting into the passenger seat of Lila's car, and shooting straight to the Waxwood Police Department.

"Tell me again why we all had to go together?"

"We were all worried about it," Lila replied. "Didn't you get the group chat invite?"

Honestly, the past few days have been a blur. I certainly didn't remember getting added to any group chat.

"I just hope the police are not going to sweep this under the rug. I could tell they weren't listening to me in my interview." Elle snarled her upper lip with distaste, "If I find out they're not taking this seriously, I'm going to be livid."

"Well, it's still too early to assume that. Uncle Wyatt is very capable and intelligent. I'm sure if there is something weird going on about this, they'll be all over it." I tried to remain hopeful but at the same time, I ran my fingers over my bottom lip, feeling out the light gashes where I had peeled the skin off earlier.

Lila pulled into a parking spot and we all got out of the car. When we were up to the door, Memphis held it for us, dramatically bowing to display his peak chivalry. Lila and I chuckled, but it was Elle's eye rolling that deepened his smirk.

In the front lobby, a desk clerk paused her typing so she could greet us, "Hello, can I help you?"

"We're here for my dad," Memphis said.

"Okay, what is his name?"

"Pfft, what is this, your first day?"

Although the thought had crossed my mind as well, I laughed nervously, "We're here for Captain Wyatt Moses. He's my uncle and his dad."

The lady eyed Memphis up and down, giving him a subtle dirty look. Ah, she caught up with the rest of the department quickly. All in agreement, likely hating the Captain's smart-aleck kid, "He's in his office. Just down that hallway."

I murmured my thanks before walking down the hall with the others. Just before we reached his door, a thought occurred to me and I raised my arm to keep the others from going in, "Wait, I don't want to come off as confrontational. I don't think that'll get us what we want.. Let me go in first and I will tell you what he says when I get out. Okay?"

There were some low, disappointed mumbles, but they eventually agreed and sat down in the waiting area.

I knocked on the door, only stepping in when he gave a gruff, "Come in."

"Hi, Uncle Wyatt." My voice was smaller than I wanted it to be. I eyed his paperwork, "I hope this isn't a bad time..."

He looked up at me and smiled, "Hey, Jenny. Nah, you're all good. Well, don't you look pretty? Why all dressed up?"

I looked down at my outfit. I was wearing a black dress with white puffy sleeves and a matching collar, paired with pearls, tights, and heeled loafers. I reached for the necklace and started fiddling with the beads when I softly answered, "I just got back from Linda's viewing."

His entire face puckered like he just bit into a lemon. His eyes tightly closed and he sucked in a regretful breath, "Oh. Shoot. I'm sorry. For your loss, I mean."

"That's, uh, actually what I wanted to talk to you about. I wanted to see what your...what your progress was on the situation. I haven't been able to stop thinking about it since it happened."

"Yeah, I get that. You've been through a lot, but don't worry. We were very thorough. We left no stone unturned."

"Oh, that's great. I'm–" I blinked once or twice. "You *were* thorough?"

He cleared his throat, "Well, it was ruled an accident. She was elderly, your coworkers say she was prone to being a little clumsy. She must have tripped coming up the stairs and she fell."

I suddenly felt a breeze behind me and realized the door had swung open. *Uh oh.* The others must have been listening at the door. I actually wasn't surprised. Although everyone had been speaking at once, Lila's and Elle's voices were overlapping, but Memphis's protests were the clearest of the three.

"I saw someone! I chased the guy myself! He had to have been right there when Linda fell!"

"I told you guys to stay in the hall," I said through gritted teeth.

The others crowded around me and eyed my uncle critically. If I didn't speak up, soon they'd keep going, "Shouldn't witnesses be enough to at least keep this open? I saw this show once and they–"

"I'm going to stop you there," Uncle Wyatt lifted a firm hand. "Criminal investigations don't work like those cop shows or mystery novels or whatever. It's a lot more complicated than that."

I clearly haven't made it very far with him. Bad start.

"Dad, look, just because you're too scared to find out what happened, it doesn't mean we–"

"Hey, hey! Watch it. Be respectful." I held my arm out to hold my cousin back. Although he's been composed this whole time, I didn't want to test his patience.

"Scared?!" Wyatt's eyes darkened. *Too late.* "It's not about being scared, Memphis. It's the fact that we don't have a good reason to pursue this any further. The closest evidence we have is what you saw. A lawyer would tear through that testimony. Eighteen to twenty year old kids talking about murder and ghost stories in a book club meeting. They'd think you just got excited and imagined all of it."

"Is he serious?" Elle muttered under her breath.

An uncomfortable silence filled the room. Lila went pale and Memphis' glare darkened to match his dad's. This was not at all how I had hoped this line of questioning would go, to say the least. At the rate Memphis was going, we'd be lucky if we didn't wind up in one of the cells. But we couldn't just give up, either.

I took a breath before trying again, "Okay, what if there was something you missed? If there was more found later, could you guys try again?"

"It's possible–but I can't be the one to do it unless there's viable evidence to follow. It would be wasting police resources to send them on a wild goose chase." He sighed and pinched the bridge of his nose.

"You know what? We've taken up enough of your time. You guys are working, just, so hard and we shouldn't be stressing you out. Ready to go, Jenny?" Elle sent me a look and then eyed the door.

Memphis muttered something under his breath, but it wasn't coherent enough to be a protest. He looked down at his dirty sneakers and shoved his hands into his pockets.

"Uh, okay..." I turned back to my uncle. "Thank you for your time. I'm sorry we bothered you."

For a second, he furrowed his brows in what looked like suspicion but it was gone in a blink. His shoulders lowered in a kind of defeat before he said, "I understand you guys are upset right now. I'm sorry about Ms. Crabtree. You'd all better get some rest. If there's anything I can do then please don't hesitate to call me."

"I will–" Before I could linger any longer, the others yanked me out the door.

"If Dad wants to be *helpful*, then he could do his job instead of taking the easy way out." Memphis snapped.

"I'm surprised Waxwood hasn't gone to rot. Are all the police here useless?" Elle added.

In a sudden turn, Memphis looked at her with offense, "Hey, hey! Watch it."

"You were insulting your dad just a second ago."

"Because he's my dad. I'm allowed to insult my dad. Not you. Shut up."

"Well, it's easy for us to complain. We're not cops. Uncle Wyatt's right. We don't know anything about his job or what it takes to be a detective. Maybe we did just imagine something," I shrugged.

"All four of us?" Lila raised a brow. "That's very unlikely."

"I just wish there was some way to know for sure." Elle folded her arms.

I looked down at the asphalt as we walked back to Lila's car, my mind going through the events of that night again. My mind was itching, like there was a detail I was missing. Then it came to me. "Wait, why don't we check the security cameras at the shop? Surely something picked up what happened."

"Okay, well, why didn't the police already try that?"

"Maybe they didn't think it was necessary?" Lila suggested, "They're so confident it was an accident. Plus, they may need a warrant or something to access the shop's cameras."

Elle cocked her head to one side. "Why didn't that security guard check the cameras?"

"You mean Sleeping Beauty?" Memphis scoffed.

"Mhm," Elle's mouth twitched into a wry smirk. "I hope that guy got fired for that."

I went quiet. I've been wondering about it myself. It was a dumb thing for him to do. It was like the top of the list of worst security guard sins you can commit, but I still kind of liked him. It made me sad to think of not seeing him around every day. Sure, people make mistakes. Maybe I'd built him up too much in my head. I tried to let it go.

"Well, whoever's job it was; now we can check the cameras ourselves. Then we can finally just forget about all this. Right?"

"Right." Lila was the only one who confidently nodded, while the other two didn't look convinced. Elle folded her arms with a reluctant shrug while Memphis just got in the car, maybe giving a grunt to show he had heard me. I think everyone knew at some level, even early in, this wasn't going to be that simple.

CHAPTER 6
GHOST STORIES

I flipped the shop's front door sign to CLOSED and locked every entrance, shaking each one five times to make sure I didn't miss anything before I joined Amelia and Olive. Getting everything we needed done to close for the day, we cleaned up our station, looked around to make sure no one got stuck inside, prepared new books for the next day, etc.

"I'm so glad business finally slowed down," Amelia commented. "Did you see how busy we were today?"

"Oh yeah," I replied, but I hadn't been listening all that intently. All day, my mind had been swimming about what the club had talked about the day before.

I let out a pained grunt as I lifted a heavy box, looking down at the newly released book covers all smiling up at me, tempting me even as my back cried out in protest. I missed James.

He used to be the go-to guy we'd call when we needed help carrying stuff.

Then I realized Amelia was still talking. "Mr. Gonzales had to add more daily tours—just can't keep up with the demand."

I suddenly tuned into the conversation again, "Because of what happened to Linda?"

"That, and the ghost rumors are booming," Olive added. "We've had a couple of kids say they saw a man wearing all white in the nonfiction section. One of our regulars complained about the sound of chains dragging and the wind whistling. Even the weekend crew is complaining about technical trouble and blaming it on the ghost."

"Isn't all this ghost stuff a bit disrespectful to Linda?" I posed, tensely. "What happened to her was pretty serious. It wasn't the work of some dead magician."

"That's what *you* think."

"No matter how much we dislike it, unfortunately, we can't stop people's gossip." Amelia sighed in resignation before tucking one of her bleach-blonde wavy locks behind her ear.

"Do you guys believe there's a ghost?" I had to ask.

"Ugh, I don't know! I just hate what happened to Linda."

Olive, on the other hand, had a more candid response. "It's totally a ghost. I was just talking about this the other day with this dude. Somebody told him that they saw a tall man towering over them. His face was blurred and he wore a

Victorian suit, cape, and top hat, but in all white. It's so spooky. I bet his spirit is just outraged by all this press. Unless he wants to make his presence known..."

"Jen, can you get a couple more boxes from the back room? I think I'm missing some nonfiction." Amelia vaguely motioned behind her, probably just trying to change the subject.

"On it." I trotted across the lobby to the door she had been pointing towards but when I went to open it, it wouldn't budge. "Is this the one you meant? Do you have a key or something?"

"Oh, sorry, wrong door. Just do the other one."

I nodded and quickly opened the correct door this time, dragging out the boxes of books.

"What is that door even for?" Olive asked, as if reading my mind.

"I have no idea. Probably more storage."

We put all the new books on their correct shelves, strategically turning the covers to face the front door where incoming customers would be. It was usually one of my favorite parts of the job. Everyone on staff loved getting first peeks at the books, but I had more pressing things on my mind.

I chewed my lip and looked up at my boss. I was running out of time. It was now or never. "Uh, Amelia, by any chance could my book club and I have an after-hours meeting? They said they were excited about the book and they wanted to try a do-over since the last meeting went...like it did."

"After-hours? We don't normally do stuff like that."
Amelia gave me a look but thought about it for a moment.
"Maybe just this once. Just don't get me into trouble, okay?"

"You got it! Thanks so much! I won't let you down."

Olive waltzed out of the staff room just in time to hear
the conversation. She cocked a brow and threw her bag over her
shoulder. "Are you serious? They're letting you break the rules?"

"That's how it goes when you're a trustworthy
employee," I retorted with a playful smile.

Olive scoffed and shook her head, causing her bleached
bangs to fall over her dark brows. She murmured something
about not finding me trustworthy but she still lazily waved
goodbye before strolling to meet the others at the back door.
Olive and Andy matched pace and exchanged words I couldn't
quite catch, but Gonzales apparently did. I heard them laugh and
receive a quick, scolding finger snap from him as they moved out
the door.

I watched them from the window to make sure they all
drove off before going to the front door and opening it back up,
letting my club members in for this unusual meeting. "I could've
checked the cameras on my own. You guys didn't have to come."

"Are you kidding? Miss out when something fun is
actually happening?" Memphis laughed, practically skipping
inside. I couldn't believe I was giving him free rein here. I'm
gonna get fired, aren't I?

"Don't make me regret this, please. My boss's trust is at stake. Not to mention, your dad would kill me if I let you get into trouble again. This club was supposed to be your punishment."

"Calm down, girly." Elle held her hands out as if to steady me. "This is still technically a club meeting, just with the bonus of a little ghost hunting."

"Or living criminals," Lila corrected.

I folded my arms in front of my chest "We better at least talk about Sherlock while we're here. If we're claiming this is an official club meeting, then we'd better actually talk about the book. Or you'll be making a liar out of me."

"Are you serious?" Memphis whined, but Lila quickly interrupted on my behalf.

"Hey, it could be useful too. Studying how a detective works and stuff."

To avoid drawing unnecessary attention by turning all the lights back on, we got out flashlights. I had an antique one in my purse, Elle used her phone, then I gave Memphis and Lila some from the front desk's drawer. It really went with the spooky ambience in a way I didn't know how to feel about.

Elle shone her phone's light around as her designer boots shuffled across the floor, "You mean that piece of fiction? I'm reading it because I kind of have to, but I wouldn't go far enough to say it's useful."

"Hey, Sherlock Holmes is the whole reason we have modern forensic technology. Before him, cops never thought of checking for clues like footprints or fingerprints. They rounded up the usual suspects and maybe talked to witnesses, but they didn't get very far. Sherlock defined what it means to be a detective." I probably used more words than I needed but I couldn't take the disrespect toward such an icon.

Condescending snickers were the only responses they gave, so I let it go after I'd said my piece. We had to focus on our current objective. It wasn't comparable to actual police work, as much as I wanted it to be so. We just had to find the security desk and get into the cameras. Elementary work.

When we turned the corner, I saw a figure hunched over the computer, causing us all to jump in unison. Our flashlights fell on the dark figure until he lifted his familiar head to face us. James. He squinted, raising a hand to shield his eyes.

"What are you doing here? Did my dad not fire you?" Elle questioned, slowly lowering her phone.

I gave her a look. Okay, that was a little harsh.

"Not that it's any of your business," James slowly replied, "but yeah, I was suspended."

"Then why are you here?" Memphis asked next.

"You guys first," James folded his arms.

There was a momentary silence as everyone exchanged glances, silently asking what we should do. I took the initiative, "Promise not to tell?"

"Jen!" Elle snapped.

"What? I trust him." I looked away, trying to hide my blush. Beside me, Lila shook her head, stifling a little smirk.

"I guess it doesn't make a difference. Not like he can tell anybody without giving himself away." Memphis pointed out.

"Exactly." It wasn't exactly my reasoning, but I happily accepted it and turned back to James, "We want to check the cameras in case there's something worth the police's time from the night of Linda's...accident...that doesn't feel like an accident. You know?"

James's brows subtly lifted. For a moment I couldn't tell if he was surprised or if he was thinking, *'Oh wow. These kids are crazy.'* Instead, he said, "That's actually why I'm here too."

"You don't think it was an accident either?"

"I...I don't know." James's eyes turned downward and he awkwardly scrubbed the back of his head, "I just hate that I fell asleep when it happened. I don't know why I did that..."

My heart hurt for him. I didn't know what was going on in his life. Maybe he'd been working hard the night before and was just exhausted. Even in the low light, I could see the dark circles under his eyes. He always looked ready to fall over. So long as he wasn't intentionally trying to take a nap, right? Or maybe he was on his break or something, I didn't know. I wanted to give him the benefit of the doubt. Before that night, he and Linda seemed close. This could have been hitting him much harder than he was letting on.

"So you're here to check the cameras too?" Lila asked. "Did you find anything?"

"Dunno yet. I just logged on." James sat down at the desk and motioned for us to come closer. He put in the password for the program and pulled up the security monitors. They displayed all of the rooms in the shop, as usual. But when he input the date and time of Linda's fall, it said, *'not found.'*

"What? That doesn't..." He tried again, only to get the same result.

"That's weird," Lila remarked with a tilt of her head.

"The ghost did it," Elle said next in that flat tone of hers; I couldn't tell if she was kidding or not.

"Maybe the police did get ahold of the footage?" I wondered aloud.

James shook his head. "That still doesn't explain why we can't pull it up now. Why would they delete it?"

No one had a good answer for that.

"What do we do now? This was the only thing we had." Elle put her hand on her hip and looked over at me, as if I was to blame.

I shifted awkwardly. "I...could...uh, talk to the IT guy on Monday? He might know why. "

There was a collective groan of disappointment. James snapped his computer off with a low grumble then pinched the bridge of his nose, trying to suppress what I assumed was anger. Bless him.

Just as we all moved toward the door, a loud, sudden thud echoed throughout the building. It reminded me of Linda's scream at the first meeting. Was this going to happen every time?

"What was that?" Elle voiced what we were all thinking.

I looked at James. "Are you sure we're the only ones here?"

"Should be," his brows furrowed. "I didn't see anything on the cameras. No one works overtime, either. Not even me."

"We should check it out." Of course Memphis would suggest something like that. Here we go again.

"I don't think that's a good idea," I still tried to reason. "We shouldn't even be here. What if it's a burglar or something?"

"You guys get out of here. I'll handle it." James opened a drawer and then pulled out a flashlight of his own.

"By yourself?"

"Well, I am the only one here trained for it."

"No offense," Memphis sneered, "but I'm pretty sure cop training trumps rent-a-cop training."

"You're not a cop," James reminded him.

"Hey, my dad taught me self-defense. Trust me, I can handle myself."

"Suit yourself."

Defying common sense, we proceeded. Curiosity beckoned us for the second time. I just prayed it wouldn't lead us to something horrific again. There was more to Linda's death than Uncle Wyatt wanted to believe, even I could sense that much. It looked like this group were the few who cared enough to look further. Where would that take us? We shouldn't even be here. We weren't qualified for this, yet we were the only ones here. If things kept on the way they were, this was going to be a very long night.

I always loved the way the shop looked, but at nighttime, it truly resembled a haunted mansion. I didn't know if this was better or worse than when the place was abandoned. The fireplace embers had long died. In front of the hearth, a few leather wingback chairs sat in a circle with small coffee tables separating them that looked like they belonged in some academic grandpa's study. The lobby was currently without a rug. The last one we had was an expensive antique but after it was stained in Linda's blood, there was no fixing it. I wouldn't be able to look at it, even if they could get the stain out. So, the bare tiled floor would have to do.

James, Lila, and I slowly moved up the stairs. Despite agreeing on not splitting up, I saw Memphis and Elle straying from the group to check out the new release section—something about making sure no one was hiding there. I wanted to protest, but I was grateful they didn't move too far from my sights.

"I don't think I'll ever see this staircase the same way again." Lila's voice was barely above a whisper.

I gripped the wooden railing that was supported by black iron beams. "Yeah, me neither," I exhaled.

"It'll get better with time," James said. "Especially when we find out how it happened."

At a time like this, I was grateful to have him with us. I could see now that he was still the guy I thought he was, still had that way of making me feel safe. We all had our reasons for wanting to look into this, but it was deeper for James, I could tell. That doubled my reasons to keep going.

I was sure we had walked every section twice. We combed through non-fiction, large print, the merchandise department, and the children's room. Had a good laugh when Memphis stepped on a teddy bear in one of the reading corners that said, 'mommy', causing him to scream like a girl.

"Ugh, forget it. Are we done here? We checked the whole building," Memphis yawned, running a hand through his fluffy hair.

I checked my phone and saw it was almost 10:00. Sheesh. Hopefully my parents didn't interrogate me when I got home; it was out of character for me to be home later than even 8:30.

"We still have the back rooms," James pointed out, "but we don't have to check there. Even if someone was in here, they could've left while we were somewhere else."

I chewed my lip as I weighed the options. We didn't really know what we were looking for, but this was the only lead we had. If we didn't find anything today, we may not ever. "I mean...it wouldn't hurt to check one more place, right?"

Lila shrugged. "I got nowhere else to be."

"Guess it wouldn't hurt," Elle reluctantly agreed.

The back rooms after-hours were the scariest parts of the whole bookstore. It didn't help that they were downstairs. During the day, I was used to seeing people bustling around and working but now the hall was dead. The walls were lined with dusty pictures, a bulletin board, and a lot of old furniture we were either moving around or about to throw away.

"Yep. Murder basement." Memphis sucked in a breath and nodded decidedly.

I had to agree. "Olive was just telling me earlier about the rumored ghost...that he wears a Victorian suit and has no face. It wasn't scary when I heard it but now it's just hitting me."

"You guys are the ones who said–hey, don't touch that!" James lunged toward Lila.

She'd gotten curious, lifting the cardboard lid to peek inside. Just as James reached to stop her, the abrupt closing of the lid managed to stir up layers of dust and caused everyone to cough.

"Great. Just great," Elle groaned as she wiped her hoodie off of any remaining dust. "Are we done here yet?"

James sighed. "Come on. I'll take you guys back to the exit."

"Stop being such a girl," Memphis leaned over to tease Elle.

"Says the guy who screamed over a stuffed animal," she replied.

"It just startled me! You're the one complaining about leaving. Don't worry, princess, I'll protect you if anything happens."

"I can't even count on you to save me from a teddy bear."

They continued bickering loudly, their voices echoing in the halls and ringing in my ears. All I wanted was to be home in bed with my Yorkie. I was tired enough without the added irritation of the two of them.

"Guys, could you please–"

A scream cut me off.

Then the lights suddenly flickered overhead.

"Get...out..." a muffled voice lowly growled.

"Hey! It's the guy! That white guy!" Memphis shouted.

The lights went out again.

James held up his flashlight, searching the shadows until he landed the beam just right. Then we gasped in unison.

There was no way this was possible.

It was just as Olive described. The Victorian suit, cape, and chains floating around a tall, white figure. Glowing, like the Hound of the Baskervilles. Looked like Barry Beaumont, but this...whatever it was...didn't have a face. A shudder trickled down my spine as I took a step backward. All the feelings from the first night after Linda rushed through me. The panic, the nausea...

James reached for the taser on his security belt. "Hey! Stop right there!"

All of us immediately scattered, except for James. Like the knight in shining armor my girlish brain saw him as he stood his ground—I stopped in my tracks. The last time we met this 'ghost,' they'd hurt Linda. I didn't want to come to work the next week and find out the same had happened to James.

I grabbed the sleeve of his hoodie, jerking him with me until he was running alongside the rest of us who wanted to live. Loud, impending footsteps told us the glowing figure was hot on our tails.

I could hear my racing heartbeat in my ears and the huffing of my shallow panting. I narrowly missed a couple boxes as my head began to pound, the adrenaline kicking in but the fear taking me out of my senses.

Out of the corner of my eye, I saw a white hand reach for my face. I let out a shriek and covered my head but when I looked up it was gone. Why did we ever think coming here was a good idea?

Memphis tried to create space between us and the figure in white. He kicked down the nearest coat rack behind us and in front of our pursuer. It helped a little, the stranger stumbled over it for a second and its light began to dim. After they regained their footing, they were glowing brightly like before.

At the end of the hallway, we pooled into the elevator. My shaky fist pounded on the 'close door' button—just as the figure had caught up with us. They grunted as they held their hands on either side of the door. My ears hurt when Elle screamed in terror beside me.

"Hey, kid!" James shouted at Memphis as he started to pry one of the ghost's hands off of his side of the elevator door.

Memphis followed his example, even taking it further and kicking our chaser in the stomach so they would stumble back in pain.

I hit the button again once the glowing white figure couldn't get in. I'm sure I didn't exhale until I saw those doors close and felt the elevator begin to ascend. Once the floor rose, I swayed, for a second worrying I was about to fall over. Once I saw the others around me, I knew I wasn't the only one.

"That was the most Scooby Doo thing I've ever done in my life!" Memphis cried as he held a hand to his rapidly rising and falling chest.

Elle wasn't finding humor in this situation right now, "What was that thing?!"

James shook his head, his dark curls sticking to his sweaty forehead, "I don't know. I don't think they're friendly."

"Oh! You think so, Sherlock?!" Memphis's voice dripped with sarcasm. He groaned and doubled over, resting his hands on his knees as he tried to catch his breath.

We all got our second wind as soon as the elevator doors opened. We sprinted to the parking lot with the speed of a herd of cheetahs as if the glowing stranger would reappear at any time.

Once I got to my car, I turned to the others to ensure everyone had found the transportation they came in, then I took one last look behind me, glancing up at the building. If I were Lot's wife, I'd be salt right now, I know. All the lights were off, so

I didn't get a good view. I could feel that the alleged ghost was watching us somehow.

"Alright, everyone good? Everyone ready to leave? I'll text you all later!" I was about to get into my car but Memphis yanked me back out before I could sit down. I was already dizzy from what I assumed was the adrenaline but thanks for that.

"Wait, wait. What's next?" He asked, "What do we do after seeing something like that?"

"Why did it look like a ghost…?" Lila stared vacantly at the ground. I don't think she was talking to anyone but herself.

"I don't know, Memphis! Tell your dad?" I turned to James, "Can we use the security footage for what just happened?"

James wiped some perspiration off of his brow as he gave me an apologetic look, "They don't have security cameras in the basement since only staff goes down there."

"So, we nearly just got killed by Casper the Unfriendly Ghost for nothing?" Elle snapped.

There was a silence as everyone took a moment to breathe and just process what happened. Every few seconds, my eyes would flick over to the door, making sure we didn't get followed. As I waited for someone to make a decision, I pulled on my car's door handle, opening and shutting it every so often, only stopping when I thought I was going to yank it too hard and fall over. I just wanted to go home before I got sick.

"We can't let this go now, can we..?" James asked suddenly but it sounded more like a statement, "Now that we know someone hurt Linda."

"That's what I was thinking." Lila agreed.

Elle made a sound between a scoff and a laugh, "Tell me you're not all thinking about going back in there. I'm not doing any more after-hours stuff."

"What? You're not having fun?" Memphis smirked, only earning her glare.

I chewed the inside of my cheek while I thought for a moment. I didn't know how anyone else had energy to keep talking about this. I was still tempted to run away and never look back, but James made a lot of sense. In just one night, we had already proved my uncle wrong. This wasn't about an old lady who had an unfortunate accident, but something big was happening, and we were the only ones getting a peek into whatever it was.

"What if we, uh, stick to what we initially planned..?" I swallowed a lump in my throat. "We came here for the security footage, right? We can't get into it, b-but the, uh, the company that helped establish Wax & Ink gave us Andy. That IT guy on —on loan. Maybe he could help us like I said earlier."

I looked around at the others to gauge their reactions. Memphis reminded me of a boxer before a match, bouncing on his toes and rubbing his hands together, ready to go.

Lila kind of nodded along like she was listening but would occasionally glance at the rest of the group too like I was, waiting to see what they thought before she gave her opinion.

Elle's arms were folded, keeping her neutral position with furrowed brows and pursed lips to silently remind everyone we were wasting her time. The only evidence that she was even mildly shaken from being chased was the addition of her bouncing knee.

"Sounds good to me," James spoke up, shrugging his shoulders. *Teehee, he liked my idea.*

Memphis raised a brow at me in suspicion. "Sure but we all got on this crazy train, I want to see it to the end. You're gonna keep us in the loop, right?"

"Uh, yeah!" I laughed humorlessly. "You think I wanna do this by myself?"

"Am I in the loop too?" James asked next. "I don't think I'm allowed at work for another two weeks."

"Well, sure! I'll add you to our group chat so you can get updates on what we find." I admit I was a little quick to get out of my phone from my purse.

"Are you sure?" He lowered his chin when he looked at me. It hurt my heart to see him look so guilty, so unsure of himself. I wonder what the police told him when they interviewed him. What Mr. Gonzales must have told him when he suspended him...

As if it wasn't hard enough saying no to those big brown eyes, why wouldn't we include him? Having a trained security guard would be super useful. He just helped us escape that weirdo inside. He was in this now.

"Hey, anybody who gets in trouble with authority is alright with me." Memphis grinned proudly.

I quickly chimed in, "Also, when we find out what happened to Linda, it'll make you look better that you helped us."

James let out a soft chuckle of disbelief. He awkwardly rubbed the back of his neck, looking over the rest of the club now. "I don't know what to say."

"Say your number so I can put it in my phone." I blurted out. Despite being tired and shaken from what just happened, that was the smoothest thing I ever said. I can't believe I pulled it off.

James took my phone and put his number in. Oh, how long I've waited for this moment. Though this was not how I had pictured it happening, I'd take it.

I scrolled briefly through my inbox until I found the group chat and I added James's contact to it. Taking a shaky breath, I remembered the task at hand. This was huge.

"Welcome to book club, James," Lila grinned.

"Go, team." Elle pumped an unenthusiastic fist. "Now can we go before that thing comes out and murders us?"

CHAPTER 7
THE GAME IS (OFFICIALLY) AFOOT

After a weekend of praying and hoping, I was at work again. I was grateful for the time to get my thoughts together. The morning after our second haunting, I overslept–my dad joked that he thought I was dead. I guess ghost-hunting takes a lot out of you.

Now I am prepared. We have a plan. There's nothing to be nervous about, I tried to remind myself as I pushed my wooden cart onto the elevator and headed up to the second floor. I was a little calmer now, seeing the building back in the daylight like Friday never happened. Or maybe that's just what I wanted to convince myself so I didn't have to face Andy. He was a nice guy, but is he going to get suspicious of me asking for a favor like this? What if he told Gonzales, would I get in trouble? I couldn't afford to think like this. I couldn't back out now.

I forced myself to try and relax as I took some books off the shelf. Once the items were on my cart, I took a duster and went over the wooden surface so it shined. I wasn't procrastinating talking to Andy, I was just doing my job.

Then there was a thud and the flush of pages. A book fell. I sighed and turned around to pick it up, but when I went to reach for it, I saw the gap in the shelf where the book used to be. In its place was a single eye staring back at me. A wide, hazel eye that was so round and unnerving, reminding me of Poe's *Tell Tale Heart* the way it just...stared.

I let out a shaky breath, my mind completely blank. Shortly after, there were footsteps. That grew quicker and louder, coming for me. My body tensed, waiting for impact–but it never came.

My cousin stood over me, absolutely cackling and clapping his hands. "Gotcha! Did I scare you?"

"Memphis! What are you doing here? You should be at school!" I gave him a punch to the arm that didn't appear to hurt him in the slightest.

"What? I took a sick day," Memphis shrugged. "I've been wanting to know about the, you know, the thingy. Our... group project, if you wanna call it that. How are we looking? Did you talk to the computer dude yet?"

"No. I've been working." I waved my hand toward the book cart to display my evidence. "I'll get to it though, okay? How about when I get out then we'll all meet and talk about it? No more skipping school."

"Yeah, yeah. Whatever."

In case he didn't feel lectured enough, I added, "Have you been reading the book?"

"Wha–the book? Now?" Memphis exclaimed incredulously. "Are you serious?"

I folded my arms and frowned sternly at him. I was completely serious. I meant it when I said I wanted us to keep reading it. I didn't want to lie when I told my boss or my parents I was going to a book club meeting.

He groaned, "Jen, the Victorian stuff is weird to read. You have to keep a British accent in your head the whole time."

"I'm sure you'll get used to it," I coolly turned around again, returning the books to their places on the newly cleaned shelf. "You're a smart kid. Just stop skipping school, okay? Or I'll find you more books to read. I just saw this one here that you dropped–"

"That's my cue to go." And with that, Memphis fled.

He had a point, though. If we were going to get the ball rolling, I needed to get up and do this. Just rip that bandaid off. Go for it. This wouldn't be so hard if I didn't have to look at this person and interact with him. If only this was the kind of thing you put in an email.

I pushed the cart to the side. I'd come back for it later. I went to the elevator and hit the B button for the basement. Right back where we met that ghost. I fought back a shudder when I heard the elevator doors open up again. I pushed on and walked down the hall to Andy's office door. I knocked a couple of times before I heard him tell me I could come in.

Andy was sitting at his desk, his pale blue eyes glued to the screen with some reading glasses on his head. His dark spiky hair was pointing in every direction. I'd talked to him several times before. He was usually friendly. Only proving it again when he greeted, "What's up, J?"

"Hey, uh, so I just wanted to ask you a question on the, uh, security cameras? I know it's not my department or anything, but I was curious if you knew why the night Linda fell, there's no footage in the security camera system of when that happened...?"

10/10 delivery, me.

He stared blankly at me for a while. The longer it took him to speak, the harder my heart would pound. Does this come off as insensitive to Linda? Did I look morbidly curious about her fall? Do I sound nosey? Does he think I was telling him that he wasn't doing his job right? *Speak, man, speak!*

He slowly took the reading glasses off of his head. "I see what's going on here."

"You do?"

"You're trying to cope." He used the glasses to point at me. "You feel weird about having your club on the night Linda died. You poor little dude. Listen, it's not your fault what happened, okay? You need to let it go."

I sighed in relief. "Okay, okay. I know it's not my–yeah. But could you please let me see the footage? It would mean a lot to me."

"Afraid that's a no-can-do."

I blinked at him. "Oh?"

"Yeah, uh, I'm sorry. Even if I wanted to, big boss Gonzales said no one could have it. He has it on his computer and doesn't want anyone seeing it." He shrugged and put his glasses back on, reclining casually in his seat as he returned to his work.

"What? Why not?" I asked, but it didn't get me anywhere. His body language told me that he was done. He murmured a few excuses and we went around the rosie, basically reiterating the conversation we'd just had. I'd been given the only answer I was gonna get and nothing would change that.

I got off work that day at 3:00pm. I tightened my grip on my car's steering wheel during my drive. Well, today was less than fruitful. After Friday, I wanted to make some serious progress and spite whoever chased us out of the building. Someone knew we were looking into this thing. What lengths would they go to just to stop us?

I stormed into the buffet restaurant where the group agreed to meet. East Fortune, it was called, just a little ways away from the bookstore, in one of the downtown plazas. Some framed pictures on the wall honored the building's past. In the '40s, it was a barbershop, in the early 2000s, it had been an ice cream shop, but in 2018, it was bought by a man named Mr. Han who turned it into what we know it today. Chinese food was my favorite, but I doubted even that could lift my spirits.

The club congregated at a table-booth combination against the wall, underneath glowing fiery-colored lanterns and some ink paintings of vaguely Chinese scenic mountains. I must've been easy to read because Lila spoke up almost immediately.

"Didn't go so well, huh? You don't look too happy," she pointed out.

"Yeah, the way your eyebrows are furrowed is making some ugly lines on your forehead..." Elle squinted at me and motioned towards her face, wincing as if in sympathy.

I just sent Elle a glare before explaining how I went to talk to Andy and what he told me. When I finished, everyone looked as confused as I felt.

"Maybe the ghost destroyed the footage then emailed Andy as Gonzales so he wouldn't let anyone see it?" Memphis suggested with a shrug, but no one seemed convinced.

"So, no one else is going to look into this, huh?" James looked down, murmuring, mostly to himself. I shared his sentiment.

"I need some food." I left to make myself a plate from the buffet, going down a long jade green bar filled with various foods, all with appetizing steam floating off of them. No matter what they had to offer, I always ate the same thing. Teriyaki chicken, bacon-wrapped sea scallops, white rice, broccoli, and pineapple shrimp. Okay, maybe my favorite restaurant could lift my spirits a little.

After Andy, everything was getting to me, but it was nice to have a distraction of a meal and good company. When I returned to the table, I knew I needed a brief pause before we talked anymore about this thing we were doing. I was developing a headache thinking about the ghost, Andy, and the cameras. Although the whole reason we came here was to talk about work—I guess you could call it that. No one was getting paid here, but it certainly felt like work.

"Thish is so gud," Memphis slurped a noodle from a plate of what I assumed was moo goo gai pan.

"You're so gross," Elle snarled her lip at him. "Close your mouth when you're eating."

"Try to keep your voices down, but have you guys seen the news?" James whispered, leaning in closer to the middle of the table. "All the local media is talking about the ghost stories."

"Yet the cops still don't want to do their jobs." After he finished his bite, Memphis opened his mouth with mock surprise.

"Well, if it's becoming an internet trend to go ghost-hunting then that probably makes us look worse. Just another group of crazy teenagers," I muttered.

"How did Sherlock get people to take him seriously even though he wasn't a professional?" Lila asked.

"Back then Sherlock was their Google. Had all the answers and evidence laid out for them." I took a sip of my soda. "In most stories, they usually open up with him impressing the people he first meets by deducing them. When they walk into the room, he can tell them where they're from, what their job is, and any fun little secrets he can pick out too."

Suddenly, James asked, "How does he do that?"

"Um." I blinked a couple times, having to adjust to the fact he was paying attention now and making eye contact. I focused on the bridge of his nose so I could regain my ability to make words. "Well, Holmes says he first looks at a man's shoes and at a woman's sleeve. If a man wears nice shoes, it tells you his status. If they're worker's boots caked in mud then he'd recognize the soil–where it's from. A woman, if her sleeve has ink then she likes to write or she could be a typist. Or if it had paint, she was an artist. That, uh, that kind of thing."

Memphis twirled more noodles around his fork, making a scratching sound on his plate. "So all evidence leads to the same thing? The girl has to be a typist if she has ink on her sleeve. She couldn't have been, like, sending out letters or something? I don't know what Brits did back then."

"Well, that's why you have to make sure you take in all the facts first. Sherlock was very adamant about having all the data before you make a conclusion. As I'm sure I've told you before, he was based on a real person. Joseph Bell, Doyle's mentor. The Edinburgh doctor used to do it all the time to his patients. He even caught a deserter because of his tattoos and the way he carried himself."

"Can you do it?" James asked, nearly giving me a heart attack. Oh great. I didn't know I was going to be put on the spot. I would've studied up before I came here.

"Uh, I'm nowhere near as good as Sherlock, but there's a couple of things I notice. When someone signs up to be a member with Wax & Ink, I can normally guess if they're going to want text message notifications or email, based on their behavior. If they're more hurried or sometimes demanding, they'll like text. They want instant notifications on anything they need to know. If they're more relaxed and go-with-the-flow then they'll want email, something they can just get around to when they feel like it," I explained. "And sometimes people will try to return books that they finished reading to get their money back or exchange the item, but I can tell if they had read the book based on how far back the binding is. If it's a paperback, it's more flexible so it'll start rolling up the more the book is opened, showing how used it is."

"Nice," James smiled. My day was suddenly saved.

"Oooh, I dare you to try right now." Memphis grinned before looking around the room. Before I could ask what he was doing, he said, "Somebody deduce something about the chick at the cash register, and I'll pay for your food."

In sync, we all turned to look at the girl at the register. She was tall and lean with dark hair pulled back into a ponytail. She had soft makeup and purple-painted nails. She was probably a year younger than Memphis. I'd seen her around before. Her name was Winnie. She was the owner's daughter and was incredibly sweet.

"She's left-handed," Elle spoke up first, the last person I expected to contribute to the game.

Lila was equally stunned. "You saw that in two seconds?"

"The way she painted her nails. The left side is messier than the right. The dominant hand always does a cleaner manicure." Elle held up a hand to show off her perfect nails. "That's why I'm ambidextrous."

"I'm not sure that's the same train of thought Sherlock would have but whatever works," I conceded. "Pay up, Memphis. You said you'd pay for her food."

Memphis groaned and dug into his pocket for his wallet, "Please don't make her head swell any bigger than it already is."

"Too late," Elle smirked. "I'll accept my reward now."

We all laughed as Memphis begrudgingly handed over the money, which she then playfully counted. This day was officially salvaged. I was happily surprised that the group picked up the game so quickly. I worried that my earlier rant had turned them away, yet everyone still seemed invested in the conversation. They seemed like they were coming around to the Sherlock stuff. It was nice, having a group to talk to about your special interests. Despite everything going on, hearing them play along and laugh made the stress of the unknown a little more bearable.

CHAPTER 8
A HISTORY LESSON

My phone buzzed. I had been dusting the shelves in the new fiction area when I was suddenly notified of Elle's message. I glanced over my shoulder to make sure no customers or coworkers were watching then hunched over my device,

> **ELLE: Hey, Jen, are you still at work?**
> **ME: Yeah, I work until close. Why? What's**
up?
> **ELLE: Be there soon**

She replied with an emoji of a devil smiling. I did not like the vibes I was getting from that message.

Today was my long shift. As I predicted, it was weird working without James being there. I became aware of how many times in a shift I walked past the security office because whenever I had run out of tasks to occupy my time, my mind would ruminate on what he was up to. Today, I also have the riddle of Elle's message. I didn't have to wonder for long, though.

I wandered out to the lobby, seeing a small crowd forming in front of the mantle and waiting for Mr. Gonzales. Most of them held cameras or little pamphlets of Waxwood on them. I didn't think our small Ohio town had this much tourism, but now we were skyrocketing in public interest. Shame it was for such morbid reasons. Though, I couldn't blame them, I myself being so obsessed with true crime and Sherlock Holmes. What was it about the human race that was so intrigued by dark things?

That's when I heard the club coming in. They were mid-conversation, discussing...who knows what.

"Excuse me. I am a minor." Memphis stepped in front of Elle as the group crossed the vestibule.

"You're 18. You're not a minor anymore."

"I am, mentally, a minor."

"Can't argue on that point."

As much as I hated to interrupt what sounded like a lovely conversation, I waved them over. "Guys! Over here!"

"Oh yes. In the main room in front of the obvious tourists. We never would have found the spot without you." Clearly Elle's been around Memphis too long because she was either feeling suddenly quippy or being with him put her in a bad mood.

I gave her a look. "Maybe you can tell me what you're doing here, then."

The only one that wasn't in the group was James, but I wasn't surprised by that. It made sense it would be too awkward for him to come into the building before his suspension was over. I was disappointed, but at least I could focus on whatever the group was doing without stopping to check my teeth and makeup.

"Elle had a good idea of what we could do while we're debating our next steps. We should take one of her dad's tours. Learn more about our supposed enemy," Lila piped up.

"Barry Beaumont? I thought we agreed that it wasn't a real ghost," I lowered my voice in case one of the tourists behind overheard. "Why do you want to learn about him?"

"That's not very Sherlock of you," Lila folded her arms with a playful smirk. "Doesn't he have some kind of quote about looking at the big picture?"

My cheeks reddened. There were quite a few about it, actually. About data—*you can't make bricks without clay,* that kind of thing. I had just told them about it not too long ago. When she threw that in my face, it was as if the character jumped out of the book and slapped me.

"I say we keep an open mind. You never know what might be lurking. What we saw was definitely inhuman..." Elle did a Catholic cross over herself with a shudder. It was kind of funny—I didn't know she was religious. It was interesting what desperate situations did to people.

Before I could say anything else, I was interrupted by Gonzales' greeting of the crowd:

"Welcome, everyone, to Wax & Ink: Historic Bookstore. My name is Timothy Gonzales, the head of this organization and it is with great pride that I get to show you all this fantastic place. Combining modern shopping with Waxwood's rich history."

"If I can stay awake during this then a nerd like you should have nothing to complain about," Memphis leaned over and whispered to me.

I chewed my cheek before I interrupted the tour defending myself. I wasn't complaining, I was just surprised they thought to try this first. It wasn't a bad idea, though. I didn't see where it was relevant, but it couldn't hurt to cover more bases.

Gonzales went on to explain the origins of the building, the battle between the town and the company to decide what to put here—yeah, yeah, already knew that. Once his introduction was finished, he showed us to the master staircase. Before we ascended, though, he pointed out the plaster bust of Barry Beaumont.

He opened his mouth to speak then paused when his eyes landed on us, "Miss Jenevieve. Elle. What are you kids doing here?"

"We just were curious, Daddy. Book club field trip," Elle held her hands behind her back and smiled innocently. "Don't mind us."

"That is, sir, if I'm allowed to be here. I am on the clock..." I motioned back towards the checkout counter, where Olive was currently playing games on her station's computer. Other than the tour, it wasn't a busy day.

Gonzales waved a dismissive hand. "No problem at all. You work here, you should know this stuff. It's nice to see the next generation taking an interest in the town. Now, ahem, where was I? Oh yes, does anyone know who this is?"

He gestured towards the bust again then leapt towards the name tag with a dramatic gasp. He reached to hide the name from the crowd, earning laughter from the group with his bit.

The bust was five feet tall while set on its Grecian column pedestal. His hair was parted down the middle with era-accurately gelled waves. He had a sharp nose, sunken cheeks, downturned sharp eyes, and a full mustache that curled on the ends.

Before I could catch him, Memphis raised his hand, "Charlie Chaplin."

Gonzales laughed good-humoredly, "Afraid not, but I'm impressed someone your age knows who that is. No, this is Barry Beaumont. Our hometown hero who gave the town its name. He was born and raised here, growing up with a dream of becoming a magician. Not just that, but an escape artist. Put him in a straight jacket, he'd escape. Lock him in a cell and throw away the key, all the same. He became such a hit, he went on to travel the world and perform for many diverse audiences he always left spellbound. Unfortunately, all reigns must come to an end. He came back to his hometown to finish his great tour with a bang. He was tied up, put into a crate, and pushed into the river. But when he didn't make it out in the anticipated time, they got horses to drag his crate out. He did not survive."

"Must not have been a very good escape artist if he didn't...escape." Memphis murmured, grunting when Elle hit his arm to shut him up.

"Beaumont was survived by his wife, Anneliese, his best friend Jonathan Cook, and his infant son, Andrew, who talked proudly of him for the rest of their own lives," Gonzales continued.

"Aww, that must have been sad," Lila shook her head. "Imagine having to raise a kid by yourself. Especially in those days where women couldn't work hardly at all."

"Are you kidding? Her husband was rich and famous! She probably lived comfortably the rest of her days," Memphis scoffed.

"I wonder what his family is doing now. If he has any living descendants..." I murmured to myself. I cringed as I caught sight of Elle's silencing glare; it was my turn to be scolded for interrupting her dad's tour.

"Isn't it the magician's spirit that haunts this place?" asked one of the tourists while others took pictures of the bust.

Gonzales looked around for a moment before leaning in and loudly whispering, as if taking the whole crowd into his confidence, "Some have said to have seen him here. This was the hotel he stayed in before his fatal act. At the time, it was owned by his close friend. Which makes sense why his spirit would be tethered here. Some claim to have seen him in his white suit and hat, carrying his famous cane. Even in death, he still seems to mystify people and keep them guessing..."

As he described what his spirit supposedly looked like, my brows flew up. I thought back to when we allegedly met him. A floating man in a Victorian suit, hat, and cane and all in white. Except I also saw chains floating around him and he didn't have a face. Gonzales was being dramatic, but it was spooky how things were beginning to line up..

"He didn't have a cane," Memphis made a face. "I didn't see a top hat either. He just looked like this bust."

"No, I saw a hat and cane..." I looked back at him.

"I don't even remember *what* I saw," Lila admitted.

"Do you kids back there need some help?" Gonzales's voice made me flinch, "Do you have any questions..?"

My face heated up. "No, sir..."

Gonzales took us upstairs next. Someone in the tour thought one of the paintings was following them with their eyes. It appeared no one could move past the haunted rumors.

Elle's dad then went on to show us some of the old memorabilia from when the building was a hotel. A room key, abandoned perfume bottles, black and white pictures, and a menu from the hotel's kitchen with funny dishes on it, like icebox cakes and cucumber sandwiches. At one point, Memphis was scolded again for trying to reach his hand into the case to straighten one of the bottles that had fallen.

I had gone years without thinking about that day Memphis, Lila, and I had snuck into this building when we were kids, but ever since Linda's death I couldn't help but feel we were regressing. Or maybe it was fate. Would we never grow up? Only now it was even worse. We'd dragged Elle into this with us. When she was twelve, she tattled on us, but here she was.

"I'm afraid that will conclude our tour. But the good news is, we're open to Q and A. Does anyone have any questions, comments, or concerns?"

"Are there only two floors?" one of the visitors seemed disappointed.

"Open to the public, yes," Gonzales replied. "We do have a basement and an attic, but that is for staff-only, mostly storage."

I furrowed my brows, thinking back on something Olive once told me: "I heard that we had an underground tunnel system. Is that connected with us or does the city keep that for their stuff?"

I thought it was a simple enough question. It was just a rumor I had heard. But the look on Gonzales' face resembled something like panic.

"No...no tunnels," Gonzales shook his head. He let out a shaky laugh then cleared his throat, "No. We've looked into the basement. Yes, it's big and there's some space that we haven't fully explored yet. Due to safety and to, uh, health, we've left that closed to the public as well. But we don't have any tunnels.

That would be...impossible. We already have a basement. To have underground tunnels would be just too deep."

"Oh, I've heard that rumor too," Lila perked up next. "Would the tunnels be more like an underground railroad or is it like a secret passageway?"

"As I've said, that's impossible," Gonzales snapped. "That wouldn't be structurally sound..." His congenial countenance dissipated for a split second. The tone he used with my best friend made me frown, "Aha, let's focus on what we know is true about the building...any other questions?"

"What's true?" If Gonzales thought Lila and I were bad then Memphis jumped in only to make things worse, "You're freely talking about ghosts. What's the big deal about tunnels?"

This got the crowd's attention. Soon there was an influx of questions, tourists raising their hands and talking over each other, with a mixture of questions about the basement rumors as well as the ghost story. Gonzales tried to keep up with it all, motioning for them to lower their voices so he could speak but he was soon overpowered.

Once the crowd started to move closer, I felt someone jerk my arm and lead me to the back and towards the staircase so we could separate from the tour group. When we were in the clear, I saw it was Elle.

"I don't know if I should be laughing or yelling at you guys," she said. "I've never seen my dad get like that before."

"He seemed kind of suspicious, didn't he?" Memphis murmured. "And a little crabby."

"I can't believe you called him out like that," Lila shook her head with a little grin she was trying to hide with her hand. "It's funny how much more passionate he is about the ghost."

"Maybe he's trying to keep it from getting divisive?" I shrugged. "They try to stay pretty neutral here, with bureaucracy and politics and such.. Don't want us talking about it at the desk. But the ghost is starting its own thing."

We would need to tell James what we found out. Not that any of it seemed pertinent to what we were doing, but who knows? Data. We always need data. On the other hand, when you get down to it, what we needed was that security footage. We could sleuth and research all day long. It was tempting to do. It would all be worthless, though, if we didn't have evidence.

CHAPTER 9
BREATHING DOWN MY NECK

Normally, I love Wednesdays. Being part-time, I get the day off, but this time, it was driving me crazy. There was too much manic energy stored inside me. I was buzzing. My hands were itching to find new clues for this situation with Linda. Inspired after the history tour, I went to my laptop and googled Barry Beaumont to find all the details Gonzales didn't tell us.

Barry Beaumont (1888-1922) was a French-American magician, and escape artist most known for his stunt performances and death-defying acts.

Beaumont was born and raised in Waxwood,
Ohio, a small town in the midwest. He used to
perform locally before getting an agent and...

Okay, yeah, this part is too familiar. I scrolled down.
Personal life, famous stunts, legacy, scandals and legends–wait,
scandals and legends? I clicked on that. The legend part was his
ghost in the bookstore, yeah, we knew that. But scandals?

In his lifetime, Beaumont was frequently
featured in the press for rumors of aiding his
friend Jonathan Cook, owner of Cook & Connell, in
smuggling alcohol during the Prohibition era.
When police tried to question him, his wife would
answer the door, claiming he was performing out-
of-town.

I wondered with a chuckle what he would've thought if
he had lived to see when alcohol was legalized again. Now that I
read about it, I was sure I'd heard about that before, but where?
Other than the tunnels we discussed on the tour. Well, other
than that 'scandal', there wasn't much online that I didn't
already know. When I'd had enough, I shut my laptop and
reached under my glasses to rub my aching eyes. There must be
something I'm missing. I didn't want to take a break, but I felt
like I was missing something. Maybe I was burnt out, or maybe I
just needed more inspiration.

I reached for my copy of *A Study in Scarlet*, where I read
the part where Watson weighed up Sherlock's strengths,
weaknesses, areas of expertise and special interests. With so

much time on my hands, I was actually bored enough to give that a try, following Watson's template. Using '*nil*' for zero knowledge, '*feeble*' for weak, '*variable*' some knowledge on the subject but not all, and '*profound*' for great. I added '*moderate*' for average knowledge. Then, I went down the line of everyone in the book club.

```
Lila Greene - her limits:
     1. Knowledge of Literature: Moderate
     2. Knowledge of Philosophy: Feeble
     3. Knowledge of Astronomy: Feeble.
     4. Knowledge of Politics: Variable
     5. Knowledge of Botany: Profound
     6. Knowledge of Geology: Profound
     7. Knowledge of Chemistry: Profound
     8. Knowledge of Anatomy: Profound
```

Doctor Watson wrote in another category for '*knowledge of sensational literature.*' I don't know what he considered to be sensational when he's already mentioned '*literature*' once. So in this case, I'd say the sensational literature was Sherlock Holmes books. That obviously applied to our situation.

```
     9. Knowledge of Sensational
Literature: Moderate
     10. Proficient in first aid
     11. Interested in Sherlock already.
Doesn't need to be filled in.
```

12. Amiable personality, overall a good team player

Memphis Moses – his limits:
    1. Knowledge of Literature: Feeble
    2. Knowledge of Philosophy: Nil
    3. Knowledge of Astronomy: Nil
    4. Knowledge of Politics: Moderate
    5. Knowledge of Botany: Nil
    6. Knowledge of Geology: Nil
    7. Knowledge of Chemistry: Nil
    8. Knowledge of Anatomy: Nil
    9. Knowledge of Sensational
Literature: Nil
    10. Brave. Helps push the group when we're scared to keep going.
    11. Has a large athletic background consisting of basketball, hunting, skateboarding, and many outdoor activities. Could be useful muscle if the situation ever came down to it. (God forbid)

Elle Gonzales – her limits:
    1. Knowledge of Literature: Feeble
    2. Knowledge of Philosophy: Nil
    3. Knowledge of Astronomy: Nil
    4. Knowledge of Politics: Variable
    5. Knowledge of Botany: Nil

6. Knowledge of Geology: Nil

7. Knowledge of Chemistry: Nil

8. Knowledge of Anatomy: Nil

9. Knowledge of Sensational Literature: Nil

10. Plays volleyball.

11. Resourceful. Has a good social status where she can rub elbows with the right people who are important in the community

12. Long-time gossip. What is a sin in casual life can be a good tool for a detective to obtain information

Jenevieve Weston – my limits:

1. Knowledge of Literature: Profound

2. Knowledge of Philosophy: Moderate

3. Knowledge of Astronomy: Nil

4. Knowledge of Politics: Moderate

5. Knowledge of Botany: Nil

6. Knowledge of Geology: Nil

7. Knowledge of Chemistry: Nil

8. Knowledge of Anatomy: Nil

9. Knowledge of Sensational Literature: Profound

10. I'm a Christian, bringing in moral code and faith

11. I play the piano

12. Working at a bookstore, I have an entire building of resources at my

fingertips for any information I may need
on any topic.
    13. As a writer, I have a creative
imagination to craft a crime and (hopefully)
untangle one too.

According to this chart, most of us aren't painted in a
great light, but as Holmes said, it's better to be skilled in a craft
than to collect a wide range of knowledge in diverse subjects.
Holmes himself wasn't knowledgeable in a lot of these subjects,
and when the club all came together, we filled in the areas where
others are not profound. As if we make up one great Holmes. My
nerdy heart lifted at the idea, but then I paused, remembering
James was now a part of the club too. Sort of. He was pretty great
so far. So I added him too.

James Shepherd - his limits:
    1. Knowledge of Literature: Unknown
    2. Knowledge of Philosophy: Unknown
    3. Knowledge of Astronomy: Unknown
    4. Knowledge of Politics: Unknown-

I scratched out what I'd begun when I fell into an
obvious pattern. I pursed my lips. Internet stalking and face-to-
face scrutinizing still left a lot to be desired as far as weighing his

knowledge was concerned. James was very reserved, a private kind of guy. Maybe that's what I liked about him. The mystery.

Then my phone rang. Expecting it to be someone from the club, I casually glanced at my screen. *'Unknown'*, the caller ID read. I hesitated. Was this a scam, a wrong number? What if it was important–like someone from work and I just didn't have their number yet? I took the chance and answered.

"Stop looking into what happened to Linda Crabtree."

My heart stopped.

"Who is this?" I immediately stood up from my seat at my desk then opened up my window curtains. Part of me expected to see some horrible white face staring back at me. There was nothing. No one was on the street, and no other home's blinds were open. I couldn't decide if I was relieved or unnerved.

"Someone looking to give you helpful advice." The distorted voice made it hard to tell if it was a man or a woman. Robotic and full of static, like you'd hear from a villain of a horror movie.

Just as the adrenaline pumped through me, the person on the other end hung up. The line went dead and I stumbled over to my bed to sit down. I held my hand to my mouth as shuddery breaths escaped my lips. I didn't want my mom to hear me or she'd start asking questions. She was already suspicious of the amount of time I'd spent with my book club, but they were the only ones who knew what I was going through right now. I reached for my phone and made a call of my own.

"Hey, can you please meet me at Brick & Mortar? I gotta talk to somebody about this. I just got the freakiest phone call."

I rubbed my hands together and took in a deep breath, unintentionally inhaling the strong scent of mothballs. I glanced over at a display case of trinkets and smaller pieces—old bottles, dolls, Swiss army knives, makeup compacts, etc. A couple of years ago, this antique shop sold me my beloved Sherlockian pipe.

"You're not going to talk to your parents?" Lila asked, picking up a frilly Victorian hat off of a mannequin.

"Eventually I'll have to. I hate keeping secrets from them. For now, though, I don't want them calling the police. Not until we have evidence to give them."

"You couldn't search the number that called at all? It was completely blocked?" Lila turned to a nearby mirror and tried the hat on.

"Yup," I sighed and picked up an apple-shaped holy water glass with a tiny cameo in the center under the bottle cap. "Wow. Check this out."

Lila leaned over my shoulder to get a closer look. "Is it a perfume bottle?"

"Well, Jesus's mother is on it, so unless it's St. Mary no.5..." I quipped and held it up for her to see. "I need this."

"You don't."

"But I need it."

"You want to perform an exorcism on Barry Beaumont?" She mirrored my look, though it was hard to take her seriously with extravagant feathers from the hat sliding over her green eyes.

"Who said anything about using this against the ghost?" I guffawed. "I just think it's cool." I moved to set the bottle down, my fingers trembling as I let it go. The bottle clattered for half a second and it fell back onto the display case, luckily not breaking. I winced.

"Jenevieve..." Lila set the hat back on the mannequin.

"I didn't break the bottle," I replied, not knowing what else to say.

The back of my mind was screaming with an ever-present anxiety that someone knew what we were up to. If they were desperate enough, they could hurt any of us to keep us quiet. I couldn't call the police, and I couldn't hide in the antique shop forever.

"Alright, come here." Lila shrugged her bag off her shoulder.

"You really don't need to–"

"Shh!" Lila took out a small silver compact with a matte black circle on the lid. Labeled with white cursive lettering, and a matching outline of flowers, "Lavender butter, good for the hands and cuticles. Wow...uh, I got here just in time. You look like you've torn your fingers to shreds. You're still doing that picking thing..."

I dodged the accusation with a joke, "Aromatherapy lotion, huh? Did they teach you that at nursing school?"

"Not like I can prescribe you anything stronger." She squinted at me then shook her head, "Yeah, you're picking your lips too, start using that lip balm I gave you last time, and keep this cuticle butter–don't argue with me. Keep it. My mom makes this stuff by the jar. Also, don't forget to wear more jewelry. Something you can fidget with that's not your skin."

It was funny to envision Lila's science-y lab tech mom making aromatherapy cuticle butter–although considering her gluten-free, organic, vegetarian-ish lifestyle, I suppose it wasn't that surprising. Lila's family really enjoyed learning about God's creation.

"What would I do without you?" I asked her with a grateful yet playful smirk.

"Have really ugly lips and hands, I guess."

When Lila finished with my hands, I took her advice and put chapstick on my lips. Soon, I'll break this habit. Eventually.

After she'd said her piece, Lila chose to change the topic to something happier she knew I'd enjoy, "Looks like James is coming into the group pretty well. He seems nice. I see why you like him."

"I'm just relieved the group hasn't managed to scare him off. I think everyone likes to talk."

"Like Elle and Memphis?" Lila smirked a little bit. "Because they do talk...loudly."

"I think Elle has matured a lot, though, since we were younger. Reality finally gripped her, maybe. Showed her the real world isn't cliques and social status."

"It's a little social status and cliques."

"We did kind of made up a clique of our own, didn't we?" I looked over an old hope chest that had book pages pasted to it like paper-mâché. My eyes widened with interest, and then promptly rolled when I saw the price tag.

"Aha, I guess we did, but when the stakes are high like this, you need a tight-knit group."

"I think that's the only reason I'm still looking into this. I'm glad I'm not alone. I hope we find the evidence we need soon."

"Me too."

Another thought occurred to me. "I don't think I got the chance to tell you how great you did with Linda. It breaks my heart we were too late, but your instincts were spot on."

"Man, I was shaking like a leaf. No matter how much training you have, it's never the same as actually being there. Then when they don't make it..." Lila's voice faded with each word, lowering into a mumble.

"There was nothing you could have done, Lila. Nothing any of us could have done. But we're trying now and that's what matters, right? Lila...?"

I don't know whether it was just that exciting for her or if she was trying to change the subject again, but I heard her dramatically gasp.

"What is it?" I went closer to where she was looking at a table. I saw her turn around with a bunch of magnifying glasses, enough for all five of us.

"We have to get these!"

CHAPTER 10
WITH PRAYERS & SYMPATHY

A couple clicks of my computer's mouse and I was clocked out for the rest of the day. I said goodbye to my coworkers, then took a shaky breath, trying to settle my fluttering heart as I wondered what the club would get into today.

I went to the back room to get my purse from my locker but just when I was nearly out the door, I bumped into Amelia. She gave a little sniffle and carefully wiped under her eyelashes so she didn't smear her mascara.

My brows knitted in confusion. "Hey, Amelia, is everything okay?"

She took out her phone and used the selfie camera to check how she looked, briefly combing through her tawny hair. "I just got back from Celia's house. You know, Linda's daughter? She's such a sweetheart, I love her. I just gave her a card and told her how much we missed her mother."

I winced at hearing Celia's name. I hadn't seen her since the viewing, and that was brief. She'd come into the bookstore a couple times. She was nice. Read a lot of those romance novels about pirates and billionaires. She reminded me a lot of her mother. Not just in looks, but she was funny and optimistic, a genuinely good person.

Just when a few thoughts were beginning to stir in my head, Amelia answered the question I hadn't yet asked: "You're off the clock so I can't tell you to do anything, but if I were you, I'd visit her too. She could use all the support she could get. Plus, it would look nicer for the shop if we all let her know we were thinking about her."

Then she just walked away. Like it was that easy. I shifted my weight between my feet, awkwardly loitering in the back doorway like an idiot.

The side of me that takes after my dad was not very good with people in mourning. If someone has a problem, I can offer advice, but when people start crying, my mind goes blank. I suddenly forget what words to say or what tone to use, so I don't sound monotonous or disingenuous. I know the universal gestures of support, like hugging, but that comes with its own pros and cons. After a moment or two, I still couldn't decide if I wanted to visit Celia. It's the right thing to do, and Amelia suggested it, but should I? I want to be there for her, but I don't believe I have the tools to help.

When I got back to my car, I texted Lila to ask her advice–maybe even ask her if she'd like to go with me as backup.

> **ME: Hey, are you busy? Can I ask for some help**
> **LILA: Sure, what's up?**

I explained the situation. Then when I saw other people in the club had seen my message too, I cringed with the realization I sent this into the group chat instead of talking to Lila directly.

> **MEMPHIS: I don't see what the big deal is. If you don't want to go then don't**

Easy for him to say.

> **ME: No, Amelia could ask me about it later and then I'll have to awkwardly explain why I didn't do it or vaguely phrase it like I just haven't gotten around to it. Either way, I don't want to be like a jerk**
> **LILA: Okay. What do you need help with when you go visit her?**
> **ME: What do I do if she needs a hug?? Like, will she initiate it if she needs it? Or will she wait for me to initiate it? Then if I do, where do I put my arms?**

ELLE: Oh wow. You are hopeless, aren't you?
ME: Does anyone want to come with me?
MEMPHIS: Sorry, cuz. I've got school and
homework today. You're the one who told me not to
skip

I could read the smirk on Memphis's face.

LILA: Normally I'd love to help you, but I
think maybe you should go with someone who knows
Linda. It'll mean more coming from someone you
worked with

That makes sense. I tried to think. Should I ask Olive to come with me? Although she wouldn't be much help to me but —then Lila added a second message.

LILA: James, do you want to go with Jen?

My heart stopped.

JAMES: Sure. Meet you there in 20
ME: Lila!!
I tried to express my shock to her without giving away exactly where she'd done me wrong. This was going to be twice as stressful! It was terrifying enough to comfort a grieving family member, but another thing entirely to go with my crush!

LILA: Fly, baby bird!

I pulled up to Celia's house, store-bought card in hand. I had already signed it but I waited to put it in the envelope until James had a chance to sign it too. I only brought the card because it was what Amelia did. I don't understand social formalities. Why a card? Can't the verbal exchange be enough to express sympathy? What's she going to do with a card? Shove it in a drawer and not look at it again for months until it's time to clean out the drawer because it's stuffed with a bunch of other cards. I got it because I thought it would help and I wanted to do something, but I didn't understand it.

I braced myself and got out of the car, immediately flinching when I heard a familiar voice say,

"Hey, what did Lila mean with that baby bird thing?"

I spun around, my cheeks warming when I saw James. I was still getting used to seeing him in civilian clothes. Today, he wore gray sweatpants and a charcoal sweatshirt that was a little baggier in style and had a jersey font 'W,' printed on it. For our town's sports team, the Waxwood Wildebeests. Despite being in comfy clothes and looking slightly disheveled, he somehow only added to his own charm. He was attractive without even trying, much to my devastation.

"Uh," I had to think for a moment to remember what he asked. "Oh! Uh, I'm not very good with situations like these. I guess she just wants me to get out of my comfort zone."

"Right."

I guess he read the messages. He could probably tell for himself I didn't know what I was doing. Before we sank into an awkward silence, I thrust the card and a pen in his direction,

"Here's a card. If you want to sign it. You can lean on my car if you need to use it for a desk."

"Thanks." James put the card on my window to briefly scribble his name.

When he handed it back to me, I licked the envelope and stuffed, sealing it shut.

"Did you see my message about hugs? What do I do if she needs a hug?" I whispered as we passed garden gnomes and a porch swing, approaching the door.

"How about you just give her the card and I'll lead the conversation?" James suggested. "Would that make it easier?"

This was it. This was the moment I knew this was the man I was destined to marry. *Yes, sir, please take care of my problems for me.* "Would you please?"

"Sure." James lifted his fist and knocked on the door.

I was surprised he offered. He didn't strike me as a chatty person. He wasn't chummy with any of our coworkers—at least, not that I've seen. Although he and Linda used to talk sometimes, I didn't know how often.

"Who is it?" A new, lighter voice asked before opening the door. Celia Crabtree. She was the spitting image of her mom. Her brown hair was stuffed into a messy bun and she wore a wrinkled waitress's uniform. She smelled like bacon grease and maple syrup. Must've come back from a shift. I grimaced with guilt. We likely stopped her from going to take a shower and relax at home.

"Oh, hello. You two worked with my mom, right? Is it... Jenna?"

"Jenevieve," James said before I could.

"Oh, right, Jenevieve."

"But you can call me Jen." My voice was croaky as I held the card out. "This is for you."

"Oh thank you!" She took it with a little laugh—maybe my delivery was a little too eager. She accepted the gift though and opened it up, reading over the factory-written sympathy message, and what we'd added to the card.

'So sorry for your loss! Will be praying for your family.'

"*With sympathy, Jenevieve Weston and James Shepherd.*' Oh, I remember now. You're the security guard..."

In the corner of my eye, I noticed James had winced at the tone she used for his work title. The nudging reminder that it had been his job to protect her. Now I felt bad for letting him lead the conversation. This was probably extra awkward for him.

Here he was, feeling guilty and uncomfortable, and I just didn't get social cues.

"I wasn't sure if you were busy or expecting company, or anything. Is this a good time to drop by?" I asked softly.

"Hmm? Oh, yes. Of course. I'm sorry. Come right in. You're perfectly fine." Celia stepped back, opening the door wider so we could walk in. "Would either of you like some tea? Maybe some coffee?"

I glanced at James first. I did want some tea but would it be rude to have her make us some? Yeah, she was offering but what if she was just doing that to be nice and she didn't actually want to go through the trouble? What was the unspoken rule on this? If James said no, I knew I'd just let his answer speak for both of us.

"Coffee, please. Black is fine."

I let out a breath of relief, "Could I have some tea, please? With lots of cream, if you have it. I like—I like mine really sweet."

"Black coffee, and tea with lots of sweet cream. Got it. Go ahead and have a seat. I'll go make our drinks." Celia stepped away into the kitchen to make them.

James and I shuffled into her dark house. The curtains and blinds were closed, there were only a couple lights on but it didn't feel like the lamps were doing their job. Hundreds of flowers were lined on the floor along the wall, likely leftover from the viewing and the funeral. There was a big piano awkwardly placed, stuffed between the tv and a recliner. Must've been

Linda's. The dust on the keys implied the daughter wasn't as musically inclined as the mother and just kept it for sentimental value.

The piano was old and upright. The head of it was littered with cards that were propped up where we could see them. More sympathy cards like the kind I'd given her. So that's what people did with them. Displayed them for a while. Did they bring comfort? To know this many people were thinking about them?

I readjusted my position on the sofa, pulling a crocheted blanket out from underneath me that smelled like the kind of perfume Linda used to have. I brought it closer to me, feeling the sudden urge to hug it, if James wasn't there beside me. Instead, I set it on my lap, wanting to keep it close anyway.

"Here you are. Coffee for the gentleman, tea for the lady." Celia came back with the cups, offering them out to both of us. "Be careful, they're hot."

"Thank you." I accepted my cup and took a careful sip.

"Sorry about the mess." Celia bent over and started cleaning up tissues around the end tables. It was so dark in here, I hadn't even noticed until she mentioned it. "I've been so busy with work and everything."

"Oh, no! It's no problem! I hope we aren't disturbing you but we—" I began, about to continue rambling but James stopped me.

"We're sorry for your loss."

"Right. Thank you." Celia pushed some of her bangs out of her face then slowly lowered herself into the recliner beside the piano. "I remember you, James. Mom used to talk about you a lot. About you both, actually, from time to time. James, she used to say, was always so tired. That he overworked himself. Jen was always nervous. That you both took things too seriously."

The way Celia glanced between me and James told me everything. I hoped the low lighting would hide my reddening face. I'd told Linda that I thought James was cute. Especially when he first got started on the job. But I had tried to keep it quiet the longer we worked together, so my coworkers didn't embarrass me. Thankfully, Linda didn't, and Celia didn't push it any further. Thank goodness.

"Your mom was nice. She used to bring me coffee or water and would ask me if I was getting enough sleep." A smile tugged at the end of James's mouth. He paused to take a sip of his cup. "I'm sorry."

"Don't be sorry—" Celia began but he interrupted.

"I *am* sorry—I was an idiot. I didn't know Linda was going to..." he didn't finish that sentence. He couldn't. "I promise you I'm never going to let anything like that happen again. If I'd known, I would've done better."

My eyes widened. This was the most I'd heard him talk in one sitting. Now I realized why he wanted to lead the conversation. He wasn't here to be my backup, it was the other way around.

"Oh, sweetie..." Celia got up from her seat and opened up her arms. *Uh oh. The hug.*

James got up, and the two embraced. If Celia wasn't old enough to be his mother then I'd be jealous, but there was no need for envy anyway. This was genuine empathy and comfort. James didn't cry, blubber, or break down like they did in the movies. It didn't last for hours, but it wasn't brief either.

Maybe I should be taking notes. I took another sip of my tea.

When the hug ended then Celia sat back down again. "My mother loved you. She would've understood it wasn't your fault. From what it sounds like, there wasn't much you could've done anyway."

James nodded, but I could tell he didn't believe it.

"She loved you. Both of you." Celia's eyes flicked over to me. "You were her favorite people to work with. She was proud of you guys as if you were her own grandkids. The hardworking security guard, and the future bestselling novelist."

Linda really talked about me that much?

"How is that going, by the way? Did your publisher say he was going to take your book?"

I shook my head. "No. He's still taking some of my short stories for the magazine, but he wasn't really interested in the whole novel."

I kept my eyes on what little tea was left in my cup to avoid making eye contact with James. Did he even know that I liked to write? Was this all news to him? Nowadays, we only talk about Linda.

"Oh, no! Sounds like he doesn't know he's sitting on a gold mine here. At least that's what my mom thought," she grinned. "I'm sure you'll find the right story. And when you do, I can't wait for a signed copy."

I laughed a little. "I'll have one ready for you."

In the corner of my eye, I saw James chuckle and sip on his coffee.

Celia smiled and looked over at the piano. She rubbed her arms and took in a deep breath, her smile fading. "I'm glad you both came. You guys and Amelia–it's nice to talk with the people my mom used to work with. Heh, I don't think it's good for me to be left alone with my thoughts. I've been driving myself crazy."

This made James look up. "How so?"

She looked back at him, her breath hitching in her throat like she was hesitating to say what was on her mind. Celia licked her lips for a moment then began, "I keep replaying in my head every phone call, every lunch date. As if there were a sign or something that this would happen. I remember the second to last time we talked, she said weird things were going on in the building. She'd hear hushed voices in the walls, hear the name *'Beaumont.'* Like the–the late magician. At first, I laughed it off, asking her if she believed in ghosts now. She'd murmur that it was nothing. Now it just makes me wonder. Especially with what the internet is saying about this..."

James and I exchanged wary glances. I had to bite my tongue so I didn't end up spilling everything to her. I wanted to tell her how we were looking into it, how we wanted to find out the truth of what happened to Linda. I had to remind myself that this wouldn't comfort her. It may even freak her out. She may tell the police so we'd stop risking our necks for this. So how did I comfort her instead?

"I'm so sorry..." I spoke slowly, being extra careful with my words. "I can't even begin to imagine how you must feel. If it's any consolation though, I know your mom is beyond the fear and confusion of this world now. She loved you so much, and she'd want you to live your life without any doubt or guilt."

Celia softened. "...thank you, Jenevieve. I appreciate that." She smiled again, gently.

This had turned out better than I'd expected it to. I was afraid I would be watching the clock, counting the seconds until it was time to go, but the conversation had actually flowed well. When we left, Celia walked us to the door, hugging James one more time and then me. She went with the diagonal hug, holding me for 6 seconds, patting my back twice before pulling away.

"Thank you guys so much for coming. It means a lot. Please, come again anytime, or see me at the Pancake House and I'll remember your drink orders. I'll even give you a discount," she said warmly. We went back and forth saying our goodbyes until she shut the door and we started heading back to our cars.

"How did I do?" I asked, my voice getting smaller. I felt like a little kid waiting for a gold star from their teacher.

James replied, much to my relief, "You did fine."

"Really?" I eyed him, making sure he was being genuine and not just humoring me. It was hard to tell because he had this distant look about him like he wasn't really tethered to the moment.

"Yeah, I couldn't tell you were nervous at all."

Okay, good, he was listening.

I fiddled with a loose string on my sweater, procrastinating digging for my keys. "Was that okay, what I said there on the end–"

"What do you think of what she said?" James's head jerked up when he looked at me, as if he had just woken up.

"Huh?" I blinked, processing the sudden question that didn't seem to relate to what I thought we were just talking about. "What-what part that she said?"

"About her mom, before she died. She said weird stuff was going on, voices and hearing the name *'Beaumont'*," James explained. He made a good point.

"Yeah, I'm not sure. It's interesting, since she ran into what could be causing the rumors. I hear so many coworkers and patrons talking about it, I get used to tuning it out. Could just be more local gossip?"

"Maybe," James murmured, looking down and getting that distant look in his dark eyes again.

I shifted awkwardly for a moment, waiting to see if he was going to clue me into what he was thinking, but he didn't. We just stood on the sidewalk, in front of Celia's fence as a gentle breeze brushed my hair off my shoulder. When the silence got to me, I finally said, "Well, thanks for coming with me..."

"No problem," James stretched and lazily scratched the back of his head. "You didn't say you were writing a book."

I was beginning to reach for my purse but then I froze. Another sudden thought of his. I recovered and laughed nervously, "Yeah, uh, yeah I am. A mystery novel, but I doubt anyone is surprised by that."

"Pfft, yeah, no. I could guess that. Why did he turn it down again? I figure you'd be like an expert on mysteries."

"From how he explained it, I can read books or watch movies but that lets me produce a cookie-cutter story. Like there's some things I need to experience for myself. Does that make sense?"

"I guess so. Well, if you do get something out there then let me know. I'd like to read your book too." James gave me a soft smile before heading back to his car.

Oh yeah. Just drop a bombshell like that and then walk away. No big deal. Like he wasn't in danger of giving me a heart attack or anything. He wants to read my book? I mean, I was never going to show him a scrap of my writing because that was too much pressure for me but it was super sweet of him to say. In the end, I was glad Lila pushed me out of the nest. I didn't fall or crash after all. As much as I loathed that she was going to say, *'I told you so,'* I still took out my phone so I could call and tell her how it went.

CHAPTER 11
HAUNTED

The bookstore crumbled back into that abandoned hotel. With cobwebs and graffiti decorating the peeling wallpaper. Suddenly, I was twelve years old again.

I was vaguely aware that Lila and Memphis were somewhere around me. I could hear their laughter echoing, distantly, pointing out graffiti or the decaying Grecian columns. Every step I walked, I disturbed the thin layer of dust on the ground, making small clouds around me. The further I went, the clouds got bigger and bigger. Lila and Memphis's voices grew fainter. This wasn't how it happened. Was it?

I heard more voices, but I didn't recognize them. It sounded like two men. Where were they? The noise was muffled, almost like they were coming from inside the walls. When they spoke, the foundation shuddered and dust trickled from the ceiling.

"There are kids in here. Should we do something with them before they find us?"

"No, somebody will be here to get them." The second voice sounded younger, maybe in his early 20's.

"Yeah, and then they'll look around too. What if they find us?"

"They'll only look if the kids wind up dead. Leave them alone. Block off all the entrances."

I don't remember hearing this conversation when I was a kid. Maybe it's been so long ago that I just blocked it out. If it happened at all. That birthday was a horrifying one, as well as embarrassing when Memphis's dad found us. The memories were as blurry as a mirage in a desert.

I went up the stairs, clutching onto the railing for dear life. When I reached the top, I turned around and the staircase trembled before disintegrating. I stepped forward to try and go downstairs again, but now there was no way.

I moved on, continuing to walk until I could find another way out. I squinted in the dim lighting and looked around, "Memphis? Lila?"

I saw a figure shaped like a person. I ran to greet it, jumping back when I saw it was the statue of Barry Beaumont. I groaned and turned around, my head spinning every which way as I looked for my friends, "Where are you guys? Hello?" Did they get caught by the voices I heard?

I didn't know which idea I hated more, being alone in here, or *not* being alone in here...

I shouldn't have turned my back to the statue. I heard the sound of pottery breaking. When I went to glance back, I gasped when I felt two stone arms wrapped around me. Barry Beaumont had broken out of the bust and pedestal, towering over me like a real, living man again.

"You couldn't just stop, could you?" His voice rumbled in my ear. "You're still just the stupid girl that came in here all those years ago."

I looked down, seeing my clothes and my height had changed. I wasn't twelve anymore, but I was back to my current age of nineteen. I wiggled and jerked around, but nothing I did could break his hold on me.

"All this to play Sherlock Holmes? Do you think he'd be proud of you? A fictional character?"

"And you're—you're dead!" I shot back, as if reminding him of what he was would make him disappear.

"Am I dead? Are you sure? Then why do I keep making so much trouble for you?" He dug his fingers into my arms. The gesture made me feel stiff, making it harder to move. What had he done to me?!

"Escape artists are slippery, Jenevieve. We're innocent when we're entertainment, but when you cross us...heh. Gambling with your own life is one thing, my dear lady, but it's another to throw your loved ones into the game." He turned me around to the middle of the floor. What he showed me made my heart stop.

Four new statues were standing in front of the mezzanine. Memphis, Lila, Elle, and James. They all looked horrified, all posed as if they were reaching out to defend themselves or stop what was about to happen. Elle's statue still had tears slipping down her stone cheeks.

"Guys!" I screamed. The longer I stayed in Beaumont's arms, the stiffer I got. Were we going to die here?

"Let go! Let go!" I shouted at the dead magician. He removed his arms from me but he laughed and disappeared. When I looked down at my arms, I saw plaster coating them. My feet were already stuck to the ground, I couldn't run even if I wanted to. I could still hear Beaumont's laughter, every noise making the building shudder. The skylight above us was crackling. The roof was going to cave in. If we were prisoned in statues, the impact would shatter us.

"Guys! We gotta get out of here! Guys!" The plaster climbed up my neck and reached my face. I was still screaming their names even as my world went black.

I felt a scratch drag across my face. Thick but small claws dug into my skin and I let out a pained cry. When I opened my eyes then I realized it was just Muffie. The poor little Yorkie squirmed and fought her way out of my iron grip. I woke up in bed, finding out I had been clutching her like a kid would their teddy bear. When I was awake enough, I let her go. She jumped to the ground and let out a little huff. She shook her fur, recomposing herself before wandering to her water dish.

I sat up and buried my face in my hands. Well, that was the single most terrifying nightmare I'd ever had in my life. This was the first time I'd ever experienced a cold sweat, but now I knew what movies and books were talking about. What was that? Was it a warning? Or was I just worked up from what's been going on?

I wanted to be relieved that the dream was over and wasn't real, but even if I wasn't turning to stone, it didn't mean we were safe. I still got that weird phone call. Someone knew we were looking into this and what if they got to us? My heart was pounding so hard and no matter how much I panted, it didn't feel like I could get enough air.

I heard a *'ding'* from my phone. I grabbed my device, seeing it was a text from Memphis saying they were going to meet up at the burial grounds in front of Barry Beaumont's grave. Everyone else was saying they were going. I slammed my phone down, then ran a hand down my face.

We should stop. We should quit. Was there any way to tell this anonymous caller that I was waving the white flag? I didn't want to do this anymore. I couldn't let more people die.

I squeezed my eyes shut, but then, I felt arms around me again. Instead of them belonging to a vengeful statue, they were of Celia—warm and comforting, healing.

"Thank you guys for coming to see me."

Her voice echoed in my memory, and I felt a peace sweep over me to chase away the nightmare. She had no idea what happened to her mom.

We were able to provide her temporary relief by showing our sympathy, but we knew the truth of what happened to her mom. Could I just walk away from it? Let her carry on believing it was just an accident? Unaware that her mother's attacker was out there?

This wasn't just about playing Sherlock or looking around like a curious child. There's something deeper here. I couldn't just walk away from it.

I reached out a shaky hand and pulled the covers off of me before making my way to the bathroom to take a shower and get ready for the day.

"Good morning, Jen," Mom called from down the hall. "You doing okay, baby? You look a little pale..."

I forced a shaky smile and nodded, "Yeah. Yeah, I'm okay. Just...had a weird dream."

CHAPTER 12
MY FIRST
INTERROGATION ATTEMPT

"I think we can rule out that Beaumont rose from the grave." Memphis commented.

Beaumont Burial Grounds was a cozy little cemetery. It was warm enough to sit outside without being too hot. It was perfect weather. I saw a couple of leaves drift to the crumbling asphalt paths dividing the jungle-like greenery that threatened to take over the whole place stopped only by the black gates holding them back.

In the heart of the grounds was a statue of Barry Beaumont. His remains were in a stone vault diagonal from his statue. Below was listed,

The Astonishing Barry Beaumont. He will forever continue to astound the people of Maxwood, as well as the world. Leaving behind his loving wife Anneliese, his best friend Jonathan Cook, and his infant son, Andrew.

I took a few deep breaths, letting reality ground me in the moment instead of letting my brain wander back to my nightmare. It helped to be with the others, seeing they weren't made of plaster or stone but were real and breathing. I didn't tell them about the nightmare. Elle and Memphis would just laugh it off, maybe tease me about letting my imagination run away from me. Lila would take it more seriously and probably ask me if I was still good to continue, but the rest of the group may just carry on without me. I decided the dream didn't change anything in reality. I just had to keep moving forward.

I took in another breath when I felt a small breeze flow over us, causing the trees overhead to rustle soothingly. Behind the leaves, I saw a cloudy sky that protected my eyes from the light of the sun. "What a, uh, what a nice day it is."

"Oh yeah," Lila nodded in agreement but out of the corner of my eye, Memphis cocked a brow.

"Is this sarcasm?"

"No."

"So, what's our next move?" James asked, sliding his hands into the pockets of his hoodie. Changing the subject before Memphis and I argued on why I liked cloudy weather.

Rather than sitting beside most of us on the bench, Lila folded her legs underneath her and rested on the stony ground. "So far, I'm out of ideas."

"We need that security footage," I muttered. "I know they said it's gone, but we got to check again. That may be our only chance."

"He's your boss. Can't you ask him for it?" Memphis lifted a cherry slushy to his mouth that he probably got from the gas station on the drive here.

"If you're so nervous, I can ask him for you," Elle offered. "I've been getting what I want out of him since I was a toddler."

Elle did have a terrific track record. Elle used to know exactly how to turn anybody against me. Did Elle break something? She said I did it, and I got in trouble. Did Elle push me on the playground? She convinced the teacher that I started the fight. We loved to argue with each other. Due to Elle's dad being an important member of the community, she won every battle.

"So long as you're careful," I chewed my lip, praying that she didn't make me regret this. "Just don't mention me. I don't feel like getting fired today."

"Have a little faith, huh?" Elle whipped out her phone and called her dad. "Everyone, just be quiet and let me work—hi, Daddy!"

"Hi, princess," I heard Gonzales' accented voice on the speaker. "How are you?"

"I'm great, thanks. Listen, my friend Jennifer—you remember Jennifer? You're so bad at names—she told me that she thinks I'm totally making up the Linda Crabtree thing. I told her I wasn't but she was all, *'yeah you are.'* She bet me twenty bucks that I didn't have any proof. So I talked to that Andy guy that works for you–he's so cute–but he said you wanted him to get rid of the footage. Is that true?"

"She's good," Lila mouthed to me.

I gave her a thumbs-up in return but remained quiet. It left a bad taste in my mouth that she was lying, but at least I wasn't the one doing it.

"I'm sorry, princess. I think he did get rid of it. I don't know why he said I wanted it gone though, I never told him to do that," he began. "He came up to me and asked if I thought he should. Something about if the staff found it, then it would be traumatizing for them to see their coworker like that? I don't remember."

"Ugh, that is so typical! I'm going to lose twenty bucks," Elle whined over the phone. "Well, thanks anyway, Daddy. Byeee—"

"Elle, wait! Listen! Don't go talking to people about this anymore, okay? I mean it. Did you say this was *Jennifer* talking to you about this or *Jenevieve*?"

My heart stopped when he mentioned my name. Just when I thought she had him wrapped around her finger. He was quicker than I thought he'd be.

"I said, *'Jennifer'*. I knew you were bad with names. Stop being so paranoid, it makes you go gray faster. Bye!" She hung up.

"He said my name. He said my name. He doesn't know, right? He doesn't know what we're doing?" My eyes widened, and I reached for my lip.

"I told you to stop doing that picking thing!" Lila slapped my hands away. "Keep yourself together!"

"Yeah, calm down," Elle rolled her eyes. "Daddy is far too busy with work to read into it. He hardly notices anything. Trust me, we're fine."

"I hope so..."

"Let's get back on track, huh?" James interrupted. "Andy lied about Gonzales wanting him to delete the footage. So, is the footage actually gone? Why did he do that with a police investigation going on?"

"What do we do next? Like, confront him or something?" Lila asked.

Memphis had been slurping on his slushy all this time but he immediately perked up at Lila's question. "Can I slap him like they do in movies?"

"There will be no slapping." I wanted to make that clear now. "I asked the first time, and I'll ask him again. He should still be working, I'll just drop by his office. Just me."

"Can we at least wait out in the hall?" Memphis asked. "If he's secretly the fake ghost or something, you could use backup."

"Fine, just don't draw attention to yourselves." For some reason, I had forgotten what happened the last time they said they'd just wait out in the hall...

Once we decided what we'd do, we carpooled to the bookstore, going through the staff-only entrance, and huddled into the elevator like sardines. Once I hit the button, we descended to the basement, awkwardly silent as we waited for the doors to open again. Well, almost silent. Memphis was still slurping his drink.

Elle eyed him. "Must you?"

"I must," he slurped louder out of spite. "Gah! Brain freeze..."

I already regretted letting them come with me. I could see it all in my head now. Andy would be behind a table in a dimly lit room. Lila would bring him a glass of water and play good cop. Elle would shine the only lamp's light in his face, while Memphis slammed his hand down on the table. Not like any of us knew what we were doing. The movies and books were our only frame of reference. Let's hope Sherlock was training this club well.

My heart sped up as we headed towards Andy's office. I was so ready for this whole ordeal to be over. What if we had him? What if Andy did it? He wanted to help promote the book store, so he dressed up as a ghost. Then Linda caught him, he panicked, then he pushed her down the stairs in a knee-jerk response. Since he didn't want to get into trouble, he deleted the evidence. Perfect. It felt right. The motive was a little iffy to me though, but I guess I'd find out the answers I needed soon enough.

Once I stepped off the elevator, I put a finger to my lips. "I need all of you to be quiet. Only come in if it becomes absolutely necessary."

"Be careful, Jen. If he's not afraid to hurt an old lady, he could hurt you too," James told me, his eyebrows wrinkled in a concerned way that melted my heart.

"Yeah, we got your back," Memphis added.

I was trying my best to be serious but their support made a smile tug at the edges of my mouth. It gave me a warm and fuzzy feeling to have a group behind me. Even Elle, of all people. None of them had to help, but they were.

"I'm sorry I'm acting so... I just want to make sure we're doing things the right way. But it means a lot that you all—"

"That's beautiful but we gotta hurry. Go!" Before I could finish my speech, Elle gave me a hefty shove.

My cheeks burned as I heard Memphis's muffled snickering. *Figures.* I groaned before going down the dark hallway. Once I hit my coworker's office, I put my serious face back on. "Andy?"

"Jenny! What's up?" he greeted, briefly adjusting his crooked reading glasses. "Have a seat."

I went to sit down in one of the chairs before looking back up at him. His lanky build, his height. Could I see him as a ghost? I cleared my throat. "You weren't totally truthful with me before."

He turned back to his computer, returning to work even as we were talking, "Heh. About what?"

"About Gonzales and the computer footage of Linda falling down the stairs."

His eyes drifted off from his computer towards me, "What do you mean?"

I thought what I said was clear, but maybe not. "It wasn't Gonzales's idea to get rid of the footage. It was yours. Why?"

"I don't know what you're talking about, but--"

I flinched when I heard Memphis behind me. "Liar!"

I spun around and saw the club in the doorway, all leaning in with interest. "Guys. What are you doing here? I got this."

"Hold on a minute," Andy rose from his chair and straightened his back. "You guys can't be back here. The basement is for staff only! You guys all need to leave or I'll tell—"

"My dad?" Elle gave him a little sarcastic wave, her long nails fluttering. "I talked to him, and he told us you brought up deleting when Linda fell. Kind of suspicious, don't you think?"

I didn't know for sure if Andy was the ghost, but right now, his face was as white as one.

"We don't want to accuse you of anything. We just want to hear your side of the story," Lila said.

Everything was going exactly as I pictured. The good cop and the bad cop. At this point, I was just relieved Memphis didn't start slapping.

At first it didn't seem like Andy was going to budge. He shook his head and let out a scoffing laugh. Then I saw him make eye contact with James. The security guard didn't say anything. All he did was narrow his eyes.

"Alright, fine." Andy held his hands up in surrender before slinking back into his chair. "Yeah, I asked Gonzales if I could delete that stuff. I didn't expect him to let me, but he did. Why do you guys care so much?"

"We will ask the questions here!" Memphis snapped, but James took his shoulder and held him back.

"You watch way too much TV," he muttered, moving Memphis behind him.

"You guys aren't going to tell anybody about this, are you?" The IT guy looked warily between us, "Not Gonzales or... O-Olive?"

"Olive?" I perked up. "Why Olive?"

He shook his head some more. "Uh-uh. I've told you enough. Just get out of here, would you? I won't turn you in, you don't turn me in."

Once we were sure we wouldn't be able to get any more out of him, we left. I had hoped talking to Andy would answer everything, but we just got more questions to take with us.

Memphis threw away his empty cup. "You guys should've let me talk to him alone."

"Memphis, we're civilians," James pointed out.

"That was an interrogation, it's what you do."

"So, what are we going to do now?" Elle asked, folding her arms as we walked along the sidewalk, away from the bookstore. "We gonna turn in Andy for deleting the footage?"

"Weren't you listening? He'll turn us in for probing him on bookstore stuff." James shook his head. "He gets a slap on the wrists for that one stupid move that got approved by the boss, but we could end up turning ourselves in."

I didn't like that imagery. Lila and Elle might make it out okay, but Memphis would get in trouble with his dad for breaking the rules again, and James and I would get into trouble with our boss. My head swimming with all these things, I reached to pick at my lip but Lila smacked my hand back down.

"We talked about the picking thing. Second time today! Play with your pearl necklace, not your lip. Now, what are you thinking?" Lila asked me.

I let out a huff and moved my hands obediently to my pearl necklace, and then answered her question, "It's weird

Andy wasn't scared of Gonzales. Like, he wasn't saying not to talk to him, but not to tell Olive he told us…"

"Who's Olive again?"

"The hippie girl who works the front desk with Jen," Elle waved a dismissive hand. "She's like this supernatural activist. Thinks ghosts have the right to tell their own story, and the store shouldn't use Barry Beaumont's mysterious death for promotion. She leaves the most annoying comments on my dad's social media posts."

"That sounds pretty suspicious," Memphis pointed out.

"Yeah, what if Olive bribed Andy to delete the evidence of what happened to Linda? Because she was pretending to be Barry Beaumont. Like he's angry that they're turning his death into a tourist attraction?" I bit my lip, looking at the others to gauge their reactions. "Or is that too 1960s cartoon?"

"Stranger things have happened," Lila conceded and shrugged.

Then James brought up the all-too-important point: "But where's the evidence?"

Silence fell…

We may have a plausible enough theory, but we didn't have any way to prove if Olive and Andy were behind this. Looks like we were back at the drawing board.

CHAPTER 13
COUNSELING

I don't understand what is so hard to understand about the order of books behind the pews. If there are two hymns then the order should be, *'hymnal, bible, hymnal.'* Evenly spaced. Then if there are two bibles, the order should be, *'bible, hymnal, bible.'* But I sat behind the pew, and I saw, *'hymnal, upside down hymnal, backward bible.'*

My right eye twitched. I couldn't stop myself; I had to fix the order. I took every book out, cleaned out any pens or crayons left inside it, then replaced the books in the perfect order, *'hymnal, bible, hymnal.'* Even space in between. Each cover facing out and right side up. *Perfect.*

I'd been so scatterbrained all morning, I forgot to grab my notebook and my pen. Taking notes was how I focused on the preaching. I got distracted too easily. Noticing someone's clothes, a spider climbing the wall beside me, babies crying–anything and everything distracted me. I don't know if it was a '*me*' thing or a *'Devil attacking me, so I didn't listen in church'* thing, but it was a thing.

Plus, this was the worst possible time to forget my notebook. Looking into who pushed Linda Crabtree consumed so much of my brain. The guilt in the pit of my stomach was destroying me. God deserved the attention, especially on the Sabbath Day. I couldn't let my work, or whatever you wanted to call it, take up all of my attention.

Lila was the only other book club member to attend church with me. I wasn't sure what James or Elle's religious views were, but Memphis hadn't gone to church with his dad for a while now. He used to go all the time, but since his mom left, he and his dad...

From what I retained from the message, the Pastor gave a great sermon on the importance of the presence of God, comparing it to when Israel didn't have the Ark of the Covenant and they were trying to get it back. He ended the message by thanking Jesus for all He has done for us, and for the shedding of his blood.

After church, I started to collect my things when I heard an older male voice say, "Jenevieve? Are you doing alright?"

I turned around and blinked a few times in surprise. "Yeah, yeah. I'm fine."

It was Pastor David. "Would it be alright if I could speak to you for a little bit?"

The way he said it reminded me of a principal beckoning his student to the office. Was I in trouble for something? Did the Lord put something on his heart to tell me? Have I angered God this morning?

I promise I'll bring my notebook for the evening service, Lord! I prayed. *I'll pay attention tonight!*

"I just wanted to see how you've been doing. I was sorry to hear about your coworker." Pastor David sat down in the front pew and then motioned to the spot next to him.

I sighed in relief as I lowered myself to sit beside him. He was only offering sympathies. "Oh? Yeah, yeah...it's sad..."

Furrowing his brow, he looked at me as if he could see right through me. And I believed he could.

"Has my mom talked to you?"

He hesitated for a moment and then nodded. "She messaged me, saying that you've been distant lately. That you haven't been yourself. Is this about what happened at work?"

I swallowed hard before finally responding. "To tell you the truth, I'm a little frustrated with my uncle. I don't feel like we're being taken seriously. Pastor, we saw something that night. And we've seen it again. Not just me, but the whole group. I don't know what it is."

The power of a pastor. Something about the position just made you want to spill your guts. Not that I thought we were sinning, but we've been fighting in the dark now for a while. I was starving for some guidance or a sign from God on what to do.

"Common sense tells me it was just a person. But, I've been having these nightmares and..." I stopped myself before I told him about the threatening phone call.

"You still won't tell your parents?"

"If my mom found out, she'd just tell me to quit my job," I laughed nervously. "I can't just turn away if something is happening there. Because..."

"Because of Linda," he finished for me with a sigh.

Guilt began to churn in my gut. I'd been struggling ever since I picked up this little project. I've never read one story where Sherlock Holmes hit a maze like mine only to meet every dead end. I wasn't sure if this was even my battle to fight.

"Do you think I'm crazy?"

Pastor David inhaled steadily. "From a practical perspective, I can't imagine pursuing any of this the way you are, Jen, but...there are many men and women of God who have felt the call to pursue God's justice. The Lord works in mysterious ways, after all. God may be carrying His Will through you, I don't know. I certainly wouldn't tell anybody to do what you're doing. I hope you call the police, but if the Lord has led you to this, He will help you process it–however that may look for you."

"But every time I think I've found a lead, I just hit a dead end," I groaned. "I don't have any evidence of...anything."

"Sometimes we don't always get the answer we want. You may be expecting results to come one specific way, but the Lord is revealing more to you than you let yourself notice. It sounds to me like you're making progress."

"You think so?"

"I do. Just because your club is dedicated to Sherlock, it doesn't mean you have to be exactly like him. If God needed another Sherlock, He'd have one. You have gifts outside of his that are just as useful."

I tried not to scoff. "Like what?"

"Well, you're imaginative, and I think you see people. Maybe not the nitty gritty details, but you know how to empathize, and you try to understand them. Your mind was designed for figuring stuff out. You're smart–but that's a double-edged sword because you overthink. Just rely on your gut. God's the One Who gave it to you."

"Thank you, Pastor David. I appreciate you being so supportive about this. Pray for us, please. Pray nobody gets hurt anymore," I asked as I moved to hug him.

He hugged me back. "Of course. I pray about you kids every night. If there's ever anything you need, just talk to me."

"Okay. Thank you again…" I murmured before heading out toward my parents and Lila, and our lunch plans. I had a lot to think and pray about. Why was it that every answer always led to more questions?

CHAPTER 14
MY SECOND
INTERROGATION ATTEMPT

After talking with Pastor, I felt it was time I confronted my fears. I just wanted this whole thing to be over. The club agreed. This was the best way. I was at work in broad daylight, nothing could happen to me here. Besides, I didn't want a repeat of my conversation with Andy. If I wanted this to finally end, I had to rip off the bandaid and go for it. By myself. I hoped Pastor was right when he said I was good with people. My track record combined with my rising anxiety at the idea of social interaction, was giving me doubts.

"Jen? What's with the look on your face? You look more anxious than normal," Olive sneered.

I felt my hands trembling at my sides. I swallowed my emotion as best I could and responded coldly, "Meet me in the back room. We need to talk."

I willed myself to face forward, storming to the back room without glancing back to see if she was following. It wasn't until I got to the room that I saw she had. I closed the door behind us. "I know."

Her expression was impossible to read. "Know what?"

"About Andy. The cameras." I tried not to show any fear but I couldn't shake the feeling that I was potentially standing in front of Linda's killer.

Olive sighed and changed her stance. She reclined against the wall, folding her arms and softening her gaze in resignation. "Fine. What do you want?"

This question puzzled me. She was confessing, right? This was a confession? "What do you mean, *what do I want*? I want the truth."

"Oh, great!" She threw her hands in the air. "You just want to get me and Andy fired, don't you? For what? What did we ever do to you? Just because we're together."

"Wait, what? Together? Like, in a relationship?" In retrospect, their behavior around each other had come off as a little more than friendly...

"What do the cameras have to do with this?"

"The cameras picked up on Andy and I sneaking out of work together. So, Andy just deleted all the footage in that timespan. Gonzales has a thing about relationships in the workplace. Why, what did you think we were doing?"

I sighed in defeat. There go my leading suspects. "Forget about it. Just forget it."

"So...you're not going to turn us in?"

"Your secret's safe." I left the room, my face burning.

I saw but I did not observe. I can't believe I jumped to such an outlandish idea that they were behind Linda's murder. I thought about everything I read from the books. About theorizing before one has data. Well, it felt like we had none. We made the facts suit theories instead of vice versa. What did I have to go off of? We didn't even have an inkling of a motive. Why would anybody kill a sweet little old lady?

Interrupting my self-deprecating reverie, I heard Amelia's voice calling for me. I turned around to see her directly behind me. Her arms folded and her weight shifted, almost awkward but still authoritative. "The director wants to speak with you in his office..."

I had a sinking feeling in my stomach. I had expected this for a while. Ever since Elle called her dad about the cameras. I nodded to Amelia and made my way down to the basement, my heels clicking with each step.

Soon, I was sitting in his office. Waiting for whatever he had to say. Thankfully, he didn't let the suspense carry on long before he announced, "I wanted to talk to you, Ms. Weston. I've been hearing that your book club has been successful, that's good. But I've gotten word that some of what you've been talking about has been potentially inappropriate."

My eyes widened in fear. What did Elle tell him? Did she tell him about our concerns?

"As you know, this book club is a Wax & Ink program. So anything that happens in those meetings is not just a reflection of you but of the shop itself. Now, I understand sometimes it's difficult to corral a group of young people, but if things have gotten out of your control then you should've come to another coworker or your manager for help." His words were neutral enough, a tapestry of professionalism, but the veins on the side of his neck and the shaking of his breath betrayed his attempt at civility.

I missed when Elle was the worst antagonist of my life instead of her dad.

"If I have to take a look into things then I will and, pending my investigation, we will decide from there what actions may need to be taken to help the book club get to–"

Before he could say anything more, his office phone rang.

It buzzed in its foundation and threatened to fall off until Gonzales picked up the device and held it to his ear. "Hello? Oh yes, I did receive your email–Jenevieve, you're free to leave."

Wow, that ended quickly.

Bewildered, I slowly got up from my seat and wandered out of his office. Safe to say, the rest of my shift was not wonderful. Tied between Olive giving me the stink eye for threatening her and now the feeling of walking on eggshells. How much did Gonzales know and what was he going to do about it? Everything we did in this case came to mind and if someone jumped in the middle of it, I'm sure we would come out looking intrusive and out of line. *Should I just start cleaning out my desk now? How did I let things get so out of hand?* I had only wanted to do the right thing, but everything was blowing up in my face.

I peered over the desk and furrowed my brows when I saw James walking in. He looked nice, with his dusty teal button-up and a muted beige tie. His hair was still messy but it always was. Desperate to see a friendly face, I made my way over.

"Dressed up fancy for our book club meeting, aren't you? Heh, you're a bit early too..."

"Talking to Gonzales about coming back to work." He adjusted his tie and chuckled awkwardly, "Maybe once I'm back, it'll help us with the...you know."

I winced, "I'm sorry. I don't think he's in the greatest mood at the moment. I think I really messed up today. I talked to Olive and it turns out, she and Andy deleted the footage because they're dating. Now she hates me because she thinks I'm a snitch. Then it all got worse because Gonzales caught wind of what we're doing and I just got chewed out for organizing a book club where we talk about *'inappropriate things.'* I didn't even know you were coming in, I'm sorry. Hopefully he doesn't know you've been in our meetings..."

I lowered my gaze to my shoes, like a guilty child too afraid to face his focused brown eyes. He had an intense look sometimes, but maybe it was just me.

"Well, thanks for the warning. I'll try to play it safe."

"I'm an idiot, aren't I?" I stopped him. "For thinking Olive and Andy were behind Linda."

His expression was softer than I expected, but his gaze was earnest.. Yep, there were those eyes again. "Don't be so hard on yourself. We all suspected them. Just relax and get through your shift. We'll figure this out, okay?"

Despite myself, I smiled briefly. "Yeah, yeah. Okay."

"Good. See you soon." He gave me a reassuring head nod before he left for the staircase.

I appreciated his matter-of-fact reassurance, but it was going to be nearly impossible to follow his advice. I didn't know how to relax after the day I had.

Sitting in our next book club meeting was like being surrounded by TVs at an appliance store, each of them malfunctioning and giving only white noise. I was frozen in my seat, staring at the floor, yet the world still numbly spun around me. Not dizzying, but blurring and foggy.

I didn't have the strength to interject, so I let the club chatter amongst themselves over our next move. While they argued, I soaked up my surroundings, trying to ground myself. This was where everything began. Paintings hung on the walls of people I didn't know. The fireplace sat with no fire. The neutral colors in the room normally had a calming effect on me, but I was beyond calming, trapped in my own brain just repeating this entire mess in my head from start to finish.

Back at the start, all I had wanted was for this to work. For me to make friends and for us to have fun. Maybe spending time with these people would inspire me with the right story to tell. This wasn't at all how I saw it unfolding.

As I returned to the conversation, I fidgeted with my copy of *A Study in Scarlet,* picking at the price tag sticker until I knew I could peel it off with ease.

Memphis set the tone for the whole discussion. "Gonzales getting on Jen is super suspicious. I bet he did it."

"Accusing Gonzales would be a mistake," James shook his head. "He's just being defensive, which is actual normal human behavior. Especially when you're accused of something you didn't do."

"Exactly! Thank you! This is my dad we're talking about," Elle's face was red with anger. "I know him. He would never push someone down a flight of stairs."

"Maybe he would if he had a good reason!" Memphis argued. "Maybe it was an accident. Like he dressed as a ghost for the rumors to promote the store, then accidentally scared Linda, and now he's just too afraid to come out with it."

I looked outside the window at the doors to make sure no one was around. *If anyone heard the things that were being said in here...hah, I could get fired.*

"Let's try to calm down on accusing people right now, huh?" Lila interjected, "We don't have enough to go on to point the finger at someone. There must be some piece that we're missing."

I should have been the one to say that. This was my book club, I'm responsible for everyone coming together and witnessing what happened to Linda. I wished I had the answers for them that they needed. But no matter how many Sherlock books I read, Sherlock couldn't give me the answer. My imagination couldn't dream up a plot like this. Though God walks with me, He wouldn't flat out give me the answer yet. I didn't know why, but He wouldn't. All we found were dead ends.

When we finished our club meeting, the store was closing. Gonzales had left earlier and the other employees who remained allowed us to leave through the back exit to the parking lot. I saw the tall, brick buildings behind the lot fall into a glowing orange haze under the dying light of the sunset.

I closed my eyes and leaned my head back, praying through my frustration that God would help me. *I don't know if I have the heart to tell my parents that I may not have a job anymore. I guess I could just focus on my writing, but...I like this building, and I'm just beginning to appreciate having a book club. Maybe it's for the best. If I left this job, we couldn't look into Linda anymore and the ghost would leave us alone.* Maybe God is lining someone else up to solve this thing for us so we don't have to.

I paused. My hands were empty. My phone was in my purse. My drink was tossed in a trash can on our way out. What did I forget? My book. My copy of *A Study in Scarlet.* It was back in the room, inside the shop. Could this day possibly get any worse?

"Sorry, guys, I have to go back in."

Everyone turned back to me, spinning around in perfect sync with raised eyebrows.

"By yourself?" Lila tilted her head.

"Yeah, I left my book in there," I explained. I preemptively headed back to the door fumbling for my key.

"Yeah, but my dad literally just got on you. Do you really want to go into work after-hours again? You don't want to wait it out?" Elle raised a brow.

"I'll tell the truth, that I lost my book. If I get fired anyway, I don't want to have to do the walk of shame back in here to get it." I opened the door, despite their worries. I had lost my ability to care at this point. Despite everyone's concern, I went inside, sighing in relief when the door shut behind me.

CHAPTER 15
THE BREAK-IN

It still felt like a walk of shame, despite being alone. My only audience in the dimly-lit room were faces on book covers, yet I could still feel their eyes burning my back while I thought about every choice I'd made up to this point.

My latest decision to come back may be my worst— because I wasn't actually alone after all. What was it about me that attracted crime?

I dove behind a shelf of large print books when I saw them. The two intruders who somehow broke through the shop doors in the short amount of time between the staff leaving and my coming back. How did these guys get in here so fast without being seen or heard? My rising panic prevented me from thinking straight.. *Snap out of it, stupid!* I've faced a ghost two times already. Why did I waste my time reading detective novels if I couldn't use what I'd learned?!

Okay, okay. Don't try to deduce. Just observe.

The building had an echo. It was easy to hear anything being said or done. They could have heard me come in. The keypad you had to enter the code into was loud enough without the noise of the door unlocking.

Where did they come from? I came in through the staff-only entrance and didn't hear the sound of glass breaking from the patron entrance (thank God for that, the main doors are so aesthetically and architecturally pleasing) So, that leaves the fire exit on the opposite side of the building. The only area that my coworkers rarely check before closing up, and without security cameras. At least none that we could tap into.

I prayed out of some miracle they hadn't heard me come in. I don't think I got my wish because I heard one burglar whisper to the other, "Did you hear that?"

"I swear if you say that one more time, I'm hitting you in the head with this crowbar. You've been getting on my last nerve, and we haven't even got to the door yet." The other hissed.

Door? They weren't going for the cash registers?

"You've seen the news, haven't you? This place is haunted." The first burglar whispered, "That magician stayed here when this place was a hotel. Do you think his spirit is attached to his stuff? I don't want to touch his stuff if he is..."

"Well, if there is a ghost then we'll find out tonight. Doesn't stop me from doing the job."

I could pull the alarm, but then the guys would know I was here, right? If they were vengeful and if they had a weapon on them, they could kill me on their way out. Or take a hostage. These guys didn't sound all that bright, but they did sound easily panicked. Especially if one of them was afraid of ghosts. Which could either be useful to me or it could make him do something unpredictable when startled.

I took out my phone, dimmed the brightness on my screen, then texted the book club. They seemed like they would wait for me, I hope they didn't change their mind. I told them about the burglars being in the bookstore and braced myself for the scolding for going back in alone.

MEMPHIS: This wasn't what we thought would happen, but why not? I could see you getting blamed for this too

I rolled my eyes. That was at the bottom of my list of worries right now. I sighed and texted back, my trembling fingers fumbling with the screen's keys.

ME: Coild u guys csll the police or smthing, pls? If they find me I dn't know what theyll do to me. Why aee we gtting so mxny damgerOUS VISITORS?!??!!

I saw three dots float on the screen where a couple of them were trying to reply. Then they stopped. I had hoped that they would call the police, but it didn't help my nerves that none of them had anything reassuring to tell me in what could be my final moments. I closed my eyes tightly and shook my head. Then I felt another buzz from my phone. Their pause in texting must have been them conspiring.

JAMES: What can you tell us about them? Tell us everything you noticed

Okay, okay. Holmes up. Here we go. I relayed the events so far, including that their aim was for some door and they hadn't gone for the cash registers.

There was another pause in the message exchange until I got two texts back at the same time from the group chat.

LILA: Hang in there! You'll be okay

ELLE: Don't die

That was probably the nicest thing she had ever said to me. I ran a hand through my hair and tried to sit tight in my hiding spot between bookshelves. The best hiding spot always had a way out. Now I just had to pray that God would keep me safe and these guys would be arrested by the police soon.

Then I thought I heard the sound of a door creaking. My eyes widened. Please tell me they're not doing what I think they're doing. If the others were going to try to rescue me or something, I am not going to be grateful. I am going to be ticked. If it were possible for me to just leave at any time, I would have done it. I didn't want them to hear the door or see me trying to leave and come after me. Maybe I could do it if I put my mind to it and just shot out of there, but fear left me paralyzed. Frankly, I didn't want these guys to get away with this. Sure, the cops could come, but they may not catch them in time. I prayed the cops would catch them.

I looked around the corner to see what was going on when I got a glimpse of the lobby. James was crouched over, slowly waddling over to the piano. My eyes widened and I shook my head at him. I slashed at my throat, subtly at first then violently. If the robbers just glanced behind, they would see him. Whatever he was doing, it had to be a bad idea.

If he noticed my warnings, he didn't show it. James pressed a button on the instrument before joining me in my hiding place. "We got a plan. Don't panic."

"If you get us caught, I'm not going to feel calm," I whispered back before flinching when I heard the piano starting to play. It went on its own, Amelia often put a disc in it and it would play music from time to time. Unless you were a regular, you probably didn't think about it.

The superstitious burglar flinched as I did when the music blasted. "You hear that?!"

"It's probably electric, idiot. Just malfunctioned. Help me open this door," the other one snapped.

I turned to James again. "I don't mean to criticize your rescue plan, but I really hope that wasn't it."

He just held a finger to his lips, warning me to be quiet.

"Ladies and gentlemen, boys and girls! Barry Beaumont!" I heard a male transatlantic accent echo through the bookstore. Either Memphis was really good at impressions, or he stole that clip from the 1950s movie about Beaumont's life. An announcer then spoke, roaring cheers were heard. Definitely a video clip.

I crawled to the other end of the bookshelf and looked behind the checkout counter to confirm my suspicions: Memphis had gotten onto one of the computers and was playing a clip from online. Once the video was on, Memphis dashed out from behind the desk and went to do something else.

Once I had seen what he did, James pulled me back to my hiding spot and wrapped his arms around me. They were the ones being obvious, yet they were trying to keep me from getting caught?!

Then the realization hit me...James was holding me. Protectively. I've read books about this kind of experience. The way he shielded me from danger. The smell of his sandalwood soap. Okay, maybe it wasn't all bad—then I heard one of the burglars trip over something in the lobby and their friend shushing them—effectively snapping me out of it. Gosh, what was I thinking? It wasn't going to be romantic anymore if they found us. This wasn't fun. Nope, not fun.

"You may be right. Something weird is going on, but I know it's not any ghost. Check it out." Then I heard footsteps echoing as the superstitious burglar came back downstairs and into the lobby.

My eyebrows raised at James. Even though the lights were mainly out, I'm sure he could see my, *'I told you so'* face. I sure hope they called the police. If they did, why aren't they here yet?! Were they taking their time or am I just impatient?

"Get out..." I heard a low moan. Now I knew for sure that it was Memphis this time. "Get out..."

I could tell he was taking a page out of that ghost's book now (sorry, pun unavoidable). If that interaction with the ghost of Barry Beaumont was beneficial for anything, it was for this moment. Though part of me wouldn't protest if he showed up again, just to get us out of this situation.

"Just some punk kid, I bet. Handle that while I try to get this door open." The brave burglar returned to his work while the cowardly one hesitantly made his way across the front of the checkout counter.

I had to lean over to see what was going on. I nearly gasped when Memphis popped up from behind the guy and roared. The cowardly burglar screamed then he passed out with a thud.

When I looked at James, he was giving me his *'I told you so'* face. I rolled my eyes and shrugged. Though I was feeling a little more hopeful, I knew we still had one more burglar to go.

I heard the sound of the brave burglar's shoes squeaking against the tile floor, moving from the lobby to our area of the building, following the sound of his business partner's screams. If I looked between the books, I could see where he shined his flashlight over his partner's limp body. When he spun around, I ducked behind my shelf.

"Alright, I've had enough," the brave burglar growled, charging to the large print section, to my horror.

My heart pounded with every step he took. *Jesus, please don't let him come this way. Jesus, please don't let him come this way. Jesus, please don't let him come this way,* I prayed in my head.

I didn't get the answer I wanted. A bright light shone in my face and I heard a low, "There you are..."

I gasped and tried to crawl back. Before I even had time to think, James sprang into action. He grabbed the heaviest book on the shelf and then I watched as he pounded it right onto the guy's head. It was now that I could see why he went into the work he did. The final burglar crumbled to the floor like his partner had.

"You guys okay?" Memphis hurried over and looked at James's work. "Wow! Not bad, rent-a-cop."

James held up the book he used with a breathless laugh. "Thanks. But where did you go?"

"Oh yeah! You guys got to check this out!" Memphis motioned us over.

I wasn't sure what could be so imperative at this moment but we followed him across the lobby to the door that the burglars had been so determined to open. It was the one that we always kept locked, I'd never been into before. We leaned in for a moment, seeing a staircase. Although cobwebs hung from the ceiling, the floors were surprisingly not dusty. *What was so important down there?*

"Thank you for coming in to help me." I finally felt like I could breathe again as the paramedics and police surrounded us for the second time at the same place.

"Yeah, good job not messing things up, Memphis," Elle agreed with folded arms and a teasing smile.

"Thank God you kids are okay! I can't believe you handled yourselves like that." My uncle went to his son and threw an arm around him, "I'm proud of you, Memphis. Do you know that? You did a great job protecting your cousin. Don't make a habit of stuff like this, though."

"Dad..." Memphis's face turned red as he awkwardly returned his hug.

I smiled softly when I saw them bonding. Thank God Uncle Wyatt wasn't furious that they had done something like that. Taking on burglars? What were they thinking? But I was proud of them too. How could I not be grateful that they came in? If I had been alone the whole time, I don't know what I would have done. Their plan, albeit unconventional, was successful.

"Miss Weston, I just got done speaking with the police." My eyes widened when I saw Gonzales coming toward me. I tensed when I remembered our earlier conversation.

"I just went back to get a book, sir. I wasn't doing anything else," I began but he raised a hand to quiet me.

"I'm glad you're safe," he told me. His jaw tightened for a brief moment after he added, "That was an awful situation. If you ever need anything, then you just let me know."

I furrowed my brows. So, he wasn't going to try to blame me somehow for what happened? Or be suspicious of what I was doing there after hours? I was telling the truth, but I hadn't expected him to believe me. Thank God he did. At least, he seemed to.

"I will let you know..." I carefully replied. To test to make sure he wasn't going to fire me for what we talked about, I added, "I'll see you at work tomorrow?"

He cleared his throat. "Yes. I will, uh, see you then, Miss Weston."

Success! Maybe this whole thing had just been a blessing in disguise. It was kind of elaborate but if this situation helped make Gonzales less suspicious of me, then it was worth it.

"I hope to see you at work tomorrow too, Mr. Shepherd. That was some quick thinking you did. Good work."

"Thank you, sir." James and he shook hands.

"Do either of you know what they came here for?"

That's when everyone in the group hesitated. Did he know about that door? Were we not supposed to know what was behind that door?

"We're not 100% sure..." I murmured. "They talked about getting into a door. They could have been trying to find where you guys kept a safe, maybe? I don't know."

"Don't worry, Mr. Gonzales," Uncle Wyatt assured. "They're in our custody now so they shouldn't cause you any more problems. Whatever they were looking for, we'll find out."

For whatever reason, that thought didn't seem to comfort Gonzales. He folded his arms and readjusted his stance. Yet, he briefly nodded and hummed,

"Yes, uh, thank you, Captain Moses. I appreciate your... being thorough."

"Always. Tomorrow, though. For now, I'm gonna take my boy home." Wyatt gave Memphis a squeezing side hug, "Let's get going."

Memphis rolled his eyes as if his dad were embarrassing him, but when they turned and it was harder to see him, I think I caught a smile tugging at the edge of his mouth.

"Aww." I shared knowing grins with Lila.

It wasn't long before my parents came to pick me up. Dad was proud of me for keeping my head and Mom was flipping out about the whole thing. It didn't take long for their advice and their words to jumble together and they'd bicker about how best to support me after what happened.

I was in another world entirely. What did those guys want with the building? Did they know what was in that room they got into? That was the one area of the building I'd never been in before. Did Gonzales know about it? Because I was beginning to think it was more important than I'd realized...

CHAPTER 16
GAPS IN INFORMATION...AND SOCKS

ME: Hey, guys. My boss just texted me and said since things got so crazy last night, I could have the day off. Do we want to meet up today?

I rolled on my side in bed, reaching over to rub my Yorkie's head as I waited for them to text back.

ELLE: Yeah, sure. Meet up for coffee?

JAMES: K don't wait up for me. I'm at the laundromat right now

ELLE: Laundromat? Do you not have a
washer and dryer?

JAMES: Not at my apartment, no

MEMPHIS: Wow, Elle. Not everyone is rich
and privileged like you

ELLE: Oh my gosh. Shut up

MEMPHIS: Not gonna lie, I've never actually
been to one in real life. Why don't we just meet up
there? We'll talk murder while we watch James
wash his dirty clothes. It'll be fun

JAMES: Pls do not do that. Just wait for
like, 5 mins

MEMPHIS: Be there soon.

He added with a winky face.

Regardless of James's protests, we met up at the
laundromat. It looked like it hadn't changed since the 70's or the
80's. Wood paneling covered the walls, the machines were all
metal and shiny. The chairs were plastic and rounded, popping
out of the floor on metal poles like McDonald's old kids' chairs.
The whole place smelled of mold and detergent, making me a

little nauseous. Oh, how nice it was to have a house with laundry machines built in. Either this change of scenery was going to be good for us, get us out of our old thinking habits and open to new ideas, or we were going to be distracted..

Memphis jumped up onto a dryer that had a sign on it, saying, *'Out of Order.'* People gave him weird looks but since when did Memphis let the opinions of others stop him? He just opened up a snack bag of cheesy nacho chips. "They have vending machines here, sweet."

"It's a laundromat," James gave him a look, "You guys need to get out more."

"Well, the one you got here is like a time capsule." Lila held up her fingers and mimed taking a picture before leaning against the window. The sign over her head blinking *'Open'* in neon lights.

James rushed to take his clothes out of the dryer and into a white basket. Clearly, he was hoping to hurry this up so we could go somewhere else. Or maybe he was trying to hide his stuff from us. Whatever he was hoping for didn't happen because, with a dramatic gasp, Elle reached into the basket and pulled out a sock.

"Look at the hole on this one! Right on the toe. James, please tell me this happened in the washer and you don't actually still wear socks with holes in them?"

"Dude, how do you not feel that?" Memphis guffawed, slowly leaning down to reach for the basket too as if it were full of hidden treasures.

James's face burned a deep crimson as he snatched the sock back. "I don't have a lot of time to go shopping."

"Yeah, you do. You're on suspension," she deadpanned. "And don't try to pull out the sad puppy dog eyes like you're so poor or something. A pack of socks is no more than six bucks. You're just lazy."

"Mm-mm. Lazy." Memphis shook his head, wearing one of James's towels on his head like a woman who just came out of the shower.

"Stop bullying him. We came here to talk about...the situation, not his laundry." I reached over and jerked the towel off of Memphis's fluffy head. He yelped in protest then pouted his lip and rubbed his head, as if I hurt him somehow.

"Thank you," James heaved a sigh of relief.

"Not that this isn't already my favorite meeting of ours..." Lila smirked, going over to the vending machine and getting herself a bottle of water, "Jen's right. We should talk about yesterday with the robbers."

"I was just thinking about that door they tried to get into," I snapped my fingers and pointed to her. "Remember at Elle's dad's tour? When we brought up the rumor about Prohibition tunnels? What if that door led to those?"

"Oh yeah! Gonzales was livid," Memphis smirked. "If that door really is suspicious, sounds like he knows about it. There's some reason he doesn't want anybody down there. I wonder what's in there."

"I would die if there was buried treasure," Lila laughed and screwed the lid off her bottle of water.

I glanced over towards Elle when I noticed her beginning to go quiet. Probably because we mentioned her dad. Memphis was right. He had gotten defensive over the tunnel rumor. He would have to know about that door, right? Why were we never allowed down there? Gonzales said for safety, but when you're in the middle of a mystery, nothing can be taken for face value anymore.

"Hey, everything okay?" My brows furrowed in concern.

Elle snapped out of her reverie and looked up at me. Her mouth opened but for a moment or two, she said nothing. Instead, she sat up from her dark teal green plastic chair and dusted herself off,

"I just remembered I got...I have chores at home that I need to finish. It's my turn to wash dishes and my mom will be ticked if I don't."

"Are you sure, princess? I didn't know you did chores." Memphis teased.

She didn't even give him so much as an eye roll. That was unlike her. She just grabbed her things and walked out of the door, the bell overhead ringing as she left.

"That was weird," Lila murmured. "I hope she's okay."

"Maybe we should meet up again later," James said, closing the dryer door when he was finished with it.

I sighed in disappointment but nodded. It would be better if we could all be together when we discussed this kind of stuff. "I doubt work will let me take tomorrow off too after they were nice enough to let me stay home today. Tomorrow I'm scheduled to fill one of Linda's shifts. Maybe when I'm clocked out, we could snag a study room. Bring takeout?"

James nodded and picked up his basket of laundry. "Sounds good to me. I'll get it and bring it over."

"Are you sure you don't want someone else to get it, James? Since you're clearly not a rich man..." Memphis motioned towards his laundry.

With a squeak of his shoes, James made a threatening step towards Memphis. He didn't raise his hands or say anything. The motion and the look on his face were intimidating enough because, in a flash, Memphis hopped off the dryer and ran for the door, snickering as he scurried out like a mischievous squirrel that just ticked off a German Shepherd.

CHAPTER 17
THE SINS OF THE FATHER

"Mom, I appreciate the ride, but please don't feel bad about the other night..."

"Well, how do you want me to feel?!" Mom let out a humorless laugh–more like a wheeze–and she gripped the steering wheel like she thought I would take it from her. "You could have gotten really hurt! I never would have expected this from a bookstore. Don't go into the building after-hours anymore, I mean it."

A sick feeling sat hard at the bottom of my stomach like a rock. If only my mom knew half of what was going on in that building. Heh, if only *I* knew half of what was going on in that building.

Later, I said goodbye to my mom and went to work. It was a faster-paced day, but we had more than a couple patrons coming in asking about the robbery. Olive and I had to check our emails for the professional response Gonzales had us use anytime it was asked,

'It was an unfortunate situation that is still being looked into. We thank you for your concern but we are still working swimmingly.' It probably sounded extra-rehearsed, but we did our best.

When work was over, I clocked out and trotted upstairs for a study room so the club could meet up again. After the weirdness the day before, I was hoping to clear some things up and get us all on the same page again. To my surprise, when I made it up there, I bumped into James first, who gave me a tired smile as he carried in the take-out bag.

"Hey! Thanks again so much for the other night. My mom and I were just talking about that this morning. I really appreciate you and Memphis coming to save me…"

"Don't worry about it. It's not like we could just let it happen."

"Well, you could have," a ripple of nervous laughter left my throat. "It means a lot that you didn't. You're a good security guard–speaking of, congratulations on getting your job back. When do you start up again?"

"Monday. I–"

"Save the chit-chat until the whole squad has pulled up, guys! At least until after I've unpacked this deliciousness." Memphis hurried over to take the bag off of James's hands.

Lila arrived shortly after, straight from school because she was scratching her wrists where she had been wearing rubber gloves in the lab all day. She came up to me at first and gave me a small smile.

"Hey, are you doing okay?" I asked when I saw she didn't look as engaged as she normally did.

"Uh, maybe it can wait until we eat." Lila cleared her throat.

I was hesitant, but tried to respect her wishes. We all started bringing out the white containers of savory-smelling *'deliciousness'*, as Memphis put it, all our usual orders. Just when we were all ready to eat, we noticed there was one more member that was missing...

"How much ya wanna bet Elle ditched us?" Memphis asked, his cheeks filled with food as he spoke.

Instead of answering, I bowed my head and briefly prayed over my food. Both because I should and also because I didn't want to address the elephant in the room. I'd already been worrying after how weird she got yesterday at the laundromat.

"Uh, I don't know. She could just be busy, it happens," Lila shrugged.

As I took a bite of teriyaki chicken, under the table, my knee was bobbing like crazy. I blurted out, "Maybe we shouldn't have mentioned her dad..."

"Oh so this is my fault?" Memphis raised his brows and leaned back in his chair, readjusting his stance.

"No, no, no–" Well, he could be harsh sometimes but, "I'm not blaming anybody. I'm just a little worried if we hurt her feelings..."

"He still could've done it. Just because it's her dad, it doesn't mean he's off the suspect list."

I glanced around the table for help on how to get my point across before we offended another member of the group. I looked at James first, but his head was down as he ate some General Tso's chicken, as if he wasn't even in this conversation. When I turned to Lila next, her eyes were on the door.

"Uh oh. Speak of the Devil."

Through the window, I saw a figure swipe past and head for our door. I had expected it to be Elle but I had the wrong Gonzales. The booming knock seconds later made me jump but he didn't wait to be told to come in. Elle's dad marched straight in, wearing all of his emotions on his beet red face, his nostrils flaring like a raging bull. Just when I thought he and I were cool again after the burglary, all of that was crumbling apart.

"Mr. Gonzales–"

"Miss Weston," his voice was strained as he tried to keep professional. "I have spoken with you about this once before. Now, I've tried to be reasonable, but if you're going to spread workplace rumors–!"

"Sir, what are we talking about? I don't understand."

"You had to bring my own daughter into this? And I see you there in the corner, Mr. Shepherd. I haven't forgotten about you."

James took a breath then slowly rose from the table. "Sir, please..."

Meanwhile, Lila and Memphis had opposing reactions. She was frozen stiff, as if she was trying to make herself invisible, but Memphis had a small smirk on his lips like he was just waiting for the right opportunity to jump into the action. Before I had to worry about any of that, I saw red and blue lights flashing outside. *Wow, the bookstore has had a lot of visits from the cops lately.*

"You called the police on a book club because we were looking for ghosts?" Memphis asked incredulously, but his expression morphed from taunting to confusion when we all noticed the color drain from Gonzales's face.

"No...no..." Gonzales murmured so softly under his breath I could barely hear him. He rushed out of the room and fled down the stairs.

"Okay, that wasn't suspicious at all..." Lila commented. "I'm assuming we're going to follow him?"

"Uh, duh!" Memphis started heading for the door. Suddenly, he halted and turned to the table to start packing up our food. "Wait! Save this for after! I don't want it to get cold!"

While my cousin displayed where his loyalty resides, the rest of us hurried to the mezzanine, leaning over so we could see what was going on. We saw the cops storm inside, but they weren't coming for the staircase, not if they were here for us. Instead, they charged straight for Gonzales. One officer read him his rights while another handcuffed him.

"Mr. Timothy Gonzales, you are under arrest under suspicion of criminal neglect."

"What is going on?! Sir!" Amelia hurried out into the foyer.

He didn't reply to her or the police. Gonzales didn't talk to anyone, invoking his right to remain silent. Probably a good idea.

"Why are they arresting him?" Memphis asked. "Is he the ghost? Was I right?"

"I didn't call anybody..." I murmured. "Who did? I wouldn't have called the police on him until I was sure."

"Not me!" Memphis held his hands up in surrender.

"Me neither," James shook his head.

"Well, this just makes everything a whole ton weirder..." My cousin let out a puff of air, his shaggy bangs briefly lifting from his forehead.

I glanced at Lila, who was staring at the situation in utter shock. It was clear she didn't call anyone either. We were all in shock. *If he was behind the whole ghost situation...I don't know.* I just expected this to feel a little more satisfying. Like a burden being lifted off my shoulders or something, but I didn't feel that. I guess this kind of stuff wasn't like in the movies.

"It doesn't make any sense..." I heard Lila mutter. "Why did we see a ghost? How did he make us...?"

I rubbed my forehead, my thoughts going in another direction. "Poor Elle. Maybe we should go check on her. I don't want her finding this thing out from the news or the police."

"Yeah. I'm sure he'll be okay and they'll let him out if he's innocent."

"What if he's guilty?" Memphis asked.

I think we all know if he was guilty then there were a lot of *'what if's'* that could carry on from there. None of us answered his question.

"Then to Elle's house, we go," James sighed. "We'll tell her what happened."

"And eat up this food," Memphis stared longingly at the grease-stained bag he hadn't given up.

We all sat in my car, stuck there for a while. I'm left to assume we were all thinking the same thing. *Who should talk to her?* None of us were all that close with her. I may have gotten off easy talking to Linda's daughter with James's help, but I had the sinking feeling I may not be so lucky today.

"Should we all just go in together?" I asked the others.

"That might overwhelm her..." James replied. "You should go in first and see how she's feeling. We'll be out here if you need us."

I hated that idea. *Just because I started the club, organized the meetings, represented the group, and knew her the longest...it doesn't mean I should have to talk to her.*

"She won't be happy..." I pushed my hair out of my face. "You remember what happened when we merely suggested her dad had something to do with Linda? She's gonna blame us. She's gonna blame me."

"She needs to hear it." Lila looked at me, in earnest. "You're the right person to tell her."

I was more than a little hesitant to tell her the truth. With our history, I didn't know where we stood. Seeing her again in this book club, we hadn't touched on our past or how we feel about it. Did she still have it out for me? Did she get over it? If she did, how much worse would she get as an adult with her father accused of criminal negligence? Wow, this was such a big leap from petty kid stuff.

I looked both ways, crossed the street, went up to her door, then shakily knocked on it. I just had to pray in my head that she would listen to reason. *I didn't talk to the police. No one else did. We're so sorry for what happened and we're here for you if you need anything...*

Our relationship has never been great. This was the longest streak of being civil to each other in our lives. Now she had a real reason to hate me. Honestly, for this, I wouldn't blame her if she didn't believe me.

The door swung open before I even had to say who I was. I opened my mouth, ready to give my explanation, but nothing came out when I saw the mascara running down Elle's face. It was worse than I thought. *How much did she know? Did she blame me already? I was too late.*

This unforeseen occurrence just ruined the script I had written in my head for how this conversation was going to go.

"What's...what's wrong? I mean–I think I know–but how...how did you find out? It's definitely not on the news yet."

Elle sniffed and wiped her cheeks before laughing. "No. I...I knew because...I'm the one who turned him in."

I was stunned. A few meetings ago, she was ready to fight anyone for merely suggesting he was behind what happened to Linda, but she was the one who called?

"Really? Um, I don't know what to say...I was worried —"

"Yeah, I think I've got an idea of how much you worry." Elle rolled her eyes and blew her nose into a tissue. After she finished, she gestured quickly with her head for me to come inside.

Part of me was hesitant. Like I would walk in and she'd hit me over the head with something hard. If she were acting nice to lure me into a trap so she could let me have it. Despite my paranoia, I looked behind me and gave the others in the car a nervous smile and a thumbs-up before walking in. At least I had witnesses.

I looked around, seeing a tidy house of mainly white furniture; white walls, and wooden beams that didn't actually support the ceiling or structure of the house, they just looked pretty. It was a modern farmhouse look, very popular in our time, not my preference, but it was very tidy and picturesque like something straight out of a magazine.

We both sat down on the firm white sofa and Elle wiped at her nose with a tissue, "I thought my dad was acting suspicious after the robber thing. So, I looked at his computer. He was the one who hired those guys."

My eyebrows flew up in shock.

"Yeah! That's how I felt. I don't know why he would do it. I-I don't care why. Maybe insurance or something. Or maybe what Memphis said was right. Maybe he was really all about the publicity, but I knew I had to tell somebody about it..."

I hadn't been ready to point the finger at Gonzales yet. I'd gotten too hurried pointing the finger at Olive and Andy, and we remembered how that went.

"It freaked me out. What if he was behind this stuff for the store's publicity? What if he found out all we knew about it and made things worse because he's desperate to keep it a secret?" Elle shook her head, "I don't know what to believe anymore! This is my dad! I can't imagine him doing anything like this, but I don't know what to believe anymore. You know?"

"Listen, Elle, I know this is hard. If you felt unsafe, then I completely understand. Now that he's in custody, the police will investigate this from every angle. If something is going on, he won't be able to hide it now." I chose my words carefully, "If he's innocent, he'll be back home soon."

"Did I do the wrong thing? What if I just sent my dad to jail and he's innocent?" Elle's eyes widened. I hadn't worded it carefully enough.

"Maybe we should save that concern for later. You got enough on your plate already." I told her.

"Thanks..." Elle sniffed, "What are you even doing here, anyway?"

"Well, you're going through a lot. I'm one of the few people who know the extent of what's going on. I didn't want you to be alone..." I didn't know how to explain something that just felt like the right thing to do.

Elle paused. *What had I said this time? Did I say something wrong?*

"Take all the time you need," I told her and awkwardly patted her arm. "What do you feel up to? Everyone else is in the car. If you're comfortable with it, I can invite them in. We got takeout if you're hungry–if Memphis hasn't already eaten it–But if you're not ready for all that, we can go."

Elle shook her head, "No, bring them in. Please. I don't want to be stuck at home with my thoughts, or else I'll turn into you."

I chuckled dryly. She wasn't wrong. "Alright. I'll get them."

"She snitched on her own dad?!" Memphis couldn't believe it when I explained everything to the team.

I nodded. "Yeah, she did. I'm glad she did what she felt was right and acted on it."

"That is messed up, man." Memphis shook his head in disbelief.

"Didn't you suspect him first?" James shot him a look.

"Yeah, but he's not my dad. We were going to get him as a group or something," Memphis muttered, his breath getting quieter the further he rambled on.

"Be nice," I warned. "She's probably beating herself up already, so don't make things worse."

"Imagine if he pays the bail," Memphis snorted. "That's going to be an awkward homecoming."

"Hopefully the police get something first," I murmured, "If he's guilty then maybe he'll confess..."

"Okay, great, let's head in, okay?" James took off his seatbelt. "Before I have to listen to Memphis anymore. His mouth or his stomach rumbling."

"Wait, wait! One more thing!" I gently grabbed his jacket and tugged him back into the car before he got out. "Nobody talk about the case, okay? Let her settle in and we'll see how she adjusts. If she brings it up, proceed with caution. Do not upset her."

After I had their word they would be on their best behavior—I only really trusted Lila and James—we all got out of the car and went inside.

CHAPTER 18
WE'RE GOOD KIDS, I PROMISE

We unpacked all of the food...again. Memphis possessively hovered, eager to help dish it out. Since he was messy, it was inevitable that little grains of sticky rice and splatters of soy sauce would scatter on Elle's clean, white kitchen island.

I grabbed the nearest wet wipe and scrubbed the mess away before I lost my mind, muttering all the while about the fact that we were guests in her home and we needed to be careful with her stuff.

"Calm down, mom." Memphis retorted, already stuffing his mouth with noodles.

"They're okay. I'll get it later if I need to." Elle waved a dismissive hand and went to sit on one of the stools at the island, "Thanks, by the way. For coming over to check on me..."

"Why wouldn't we?" Lila asked, "You are a part of our group. We're all in this together."

"Well, I'm not always the sweetest," she admitted. "Or the easiest to be around."

"That's what makes us such good people," Memphis slid her plate over to her.

For the first time, Elle gave a light chuckle at one of his jokes. She looked up at him and playfully replied, "Then I must be a saint for putting up with you."

"There she is!" Memphis pointed at her and laughed heartily, "There's the Elle Gonzales I know!"

We ended up just hanging out the rest of the day at Elle's house. James and I ate while watching Elle throw little balls of paper at Memphis, who tried to catch them with his chopsticks. Lila took a phone call in the other room, and then when she came back we all moved to the living room to attempt to agree on a movie to watch. Naturally, I made the argument that whatever we watched should be one of the many Sherlock adaptations. Many groaned and protested but when I asked them if they'd rather talk about the book, they suddenly didn't want to argue anymore. Though I was grateful for that and I didn't want to pressure Elle into talking anymore about the case—especially if we had pointed the finger at the right guy—but the back of my mind was still nagging me.

Did we get the right guy? What about the phone calls I was getting? What was in that back room the burglars opened? Why did Gonzales hire them at all? Why did we see a ghost? Twice? Was this another publicity stunt arranged by my boss? Or something deeper?

After the movie, we all agreed it was getting late. Elle reassured us her mom should be coming home soon, so she wouldn't be alone for long. She thanked us for coming a couple more times then we left. Lila and I dropped the guys off at their cars back at the bookshop when she gave me a curious look and lowered her voice.

"Now that it's just you and me…" Lila began, "Do you remember how I took leftovers from the party at book club?"

I cringed. "Oh, Lila, I don't know if that's still good after a couple of weeks…"

"Yeah, well, it was nasty in more ways than one," Lila lifted both eyebrows. "My mom tried it and…she may have gotten…sick? In a way?"

"Sick? How?" I furrowed my brows.

She had me park as soon as a spot was available; whatever this was, it couldn't wait any longer. We both glanced around to make sure no one else was around, and then Lila continued,

"It made her nauseous, confused, and…it made her hallucinate. Just a tiny bit," Lila chuckled nervously. "So, as you can imagine, she had a lot of questions for me about what went down at book club. She tested the food and she found out that we were drugged."

Drugged? That word made my head spin. That was impossible. It had to be some kind of mistake. Did some medicine get mixed in? Did another bottle spill into the leftovers? Did she just get a little sick and that was the last thing she ate?

"She...tested it...?"

"Yeah. I ended up having to tell her a little of what we've been doing. Somebody drugged us. I was going to tell you earlier, but then the whole Gonzales thing started up..." Lila chewed her lip. "Maybe he did it...? I don't know. It's a lot to think about."

I gave her a double take and my face got warm. This wasn't an accident. Somebody did this to us. I haven't even taken a sip of alcohol all my life, and somebody spiked our food?! Who would do something like that?! I was just trying to have a simple book club and someone pulled a stunt like this?! Part of me wondered if it was some big joke.

I shook my head and ran a hand through my hair. "I cannot believe this. Are-are you sure? Is she sure? How...how would that happen? Maybe it was an accident? Should I call the catering service? Did they—I don't know, mix up our order?"

"Jenevieve," Lila stated plainly, putting her hand on my arm until I froze.

She didn't say anything else. We just sat there for a moment or two, until I processed what this meant. This wasn't a mistake, and it wasn't a joke. I was speechless.

"That must have been why we thought we saw a ghost," Lila started again, her voice softer this time. "The drug made us hallucinate a more ethereal, mysterious figure than what was actually there."

I don't know why I was surprised. We knew someone was targeting us for whatever reason. I didn't believe in ghosts, so it makes sense we didn't actually see a spirit coming for us. Who was actually standing there? Why did they look so weird when they came after us? I had so many questions.

"W-what about the second time?" I turned to her again, "We didn't have anything to eat that night."

"I'm not 100% on that yet, but substances don't always come in the same forms. It can also be sniffed or smoked? So, if it's in the general area somehow...?"

"Someone had to have done that to us intentionally," I said softly.

"That is what I would go with, yeah."

"This is insane," I muttered. "Absolutely insane."

This would have been a good time to tell my parents. Actually, I should've told them a while ago. I imagined my dad would have had a lot of jokes to make about the drugs at a book club. *It was supposed to be a harmless get-together! Why am I making my case already?* I didn't do anything wrong! Well, other than trespassing but that was like a misdemeanor, right? Slap on the wrists? Just thinking about getting caught in the things we've been doing made me feel even sicker. I didn't want to believe any of this was true; it was like one big nightmare.

"We're just kids." My voice came out hoarser and weaker than a whisper, "Who would want to drug us?"

Lila shrugged. "Whoever was behind the ghostly hallucination, I guess. You see how easy it was to freak out two sober burglars in the shop. Just some old audio and someone sneaking around made the one guy lose it. Imagine how much easier it would be if you drugged their food. Even just a little bit. It wouldn't take much just to cause subtle side effects."

"What about James?" I gasped when a thought occurred to me, "What if that was why he was asleep when Linda fell? He got drugged too and he passed out?"

Lila nodded slowly. "You see what I mean?"

I slid my hands up and down the steering wheel. I was suddenly eager to get on the road again, heading for the safety of home. "What do we do? Do we tell somebody?"

"Not yet. Let's just see what happens with Gonzales and the police. I want to see where that goes. Maybe we'll get lucky and he was behind it. Then all this can stop."

I wasn't convinced that was true. Our problems were just beginning.

CHAPTER 19
A TURN FOR THE WORSE

It was–unfortunately– a sunny day. I reached up to the ceiling of the car and pulled down the visor to shield my eyes from the offensive light that had burned into my vision since I was a kid. Not many people shared my opinion on that though. Because the "nice" weather had brought everyone outside, making the traffic crazy.

At that point, I kind of regretted insisting I drove while we were out. Mom sat on the passenger side, sticking close beside me, still on her overprotective kick. The burglar situation was still shaking her. Despite her helicopter parenting I had grown accustomed to, I had to keep swallowing the lump in my throat that wanted to spill out and confess everything we'd been doing at our meetings. As well as my worries about whoever had drugged us. I was still struggling to accept that.

"Hey, how did last night go? Did Elle behave herself?" I had been so lost in my head, it startled me when she spoke.

"Yeah. Elle was fine." My hands gripped the steering wheel, "She's going through a lot right now. You know, with her dad getting arrested. I think our being there really helped her out. She said she appreciated how nice we were being to her. I had a good time, surprisingly."

"Oh, praise God. I prayed about you two. You never know. Some people can change. I knew this bully who used to beat me up in the 4th grade and..." My mom went into a story from her childhood. I was listening, to begin with, but then I glanced into my rearview and saw a black car with no front license plate trailing behind me. Riding on my bumper.

"Somebody's a little too close to me..." I murmured.

"Probably somebody who is in a hurry." Mom waved a dismissive hand. "He can't go any faster. Let him do whatever he wants."

A bad feeling filled my gut. The figure in the car wore sunglasses and a face mask, and if that didn't make it hard enough to tell who it was, their car visor left a shadow over their face. That anonymous call came to mind, and the distorted memory of Beaumont's ghost.

In a panic, I swerved right without putting on my blinker and I sped up to lose them. My mom let out a scream and the ice in her tea sloshed around in protest, "Jenevieve! Slow down! What are you doing?!"

"This guy is following me."

"You're acting like a crazy person! Are you trying to get us killed!?"

Another voice said in the back of my head that I could get arrested if I caused an accident. *Let the police come. I wish they would,* I thought to myself. If I was being followed, I'd love to see who was tailing me, come and talk to the police. When I looked in the rearview, the car sped up to keep pursuing me. With another jerk of the wheel, I took a sudden U-turn and went in the opposite direction.

"JENEVIEVE!" Mom cried out again, "That was highly illegal!"

"This guy murdering me is illegal too!" I shot back, my eyes on the rear-view mirror where my stalker had copied my actions, "See? They're turning around!"

"What?" My mom glanced behind. "Why would anybody be trying to follow you this badly? If he thought you were pretty, that's one thing. But–!!"

I went quiet. How had things gotten this intense?

"Jenevieve..." Mom's tone lowered. "Is there a reason this guy is following you so diligently?"

I swallowed that lump in my throat again and tried to think of how to get around the question without lying.

"You got quiet, Jenevieve..." Mom's eye twitched and she did that thing where her underbite chewed into her top lip, making her look like a growling bulldog. "What is going on?"

"Can we talk about this another time--" I saw in my rearview mirror that my stalker had suddenly taken a turn behind me, deciding to leave me alone now. Guess they felt like they had gotten their message across.

'Stop looking into things. You've been warned.' It was spelled out quite clearly. It just infuriated me that my mom had to be here for this.

"Pull over. I want to talk about this. Right. Now."

So, I told her what the club had been doing for the past couple of weeks. Then how that led to getting chased out by what looked like a ghost, getting mysterious phone calls, almost losing my job, Mr. Gonzales getting arrested, and even the drugs. *Gosh, I feel like an addict and the drugs weren't even my fault.* I was addicted to something much more potent. Adrenaline, apparently.

"I wanted to tell you and dad about it...I just didn't know how," I admitted, my nails digging into my cuticles until they threatened to bleed.

"Jenevieve, this is insane." She didn't mince words at all. "Do you know that? Your uncle is the captain of police. He could have handled this."

"There was a case here and he didn't see it!" I looked up to meet her eyes. "Someone doesn't want this out in the open, or else I wouldn't be threatened and followed. I'm doing something right."

"If it leads to you getting murdered, it's not right," My mom snapped. "Did you stop to think how I would feel if my baby girl was found dead in a gutter somewhere? I had no idea you and your friends were doing anything so reckless. You could have died and I never would have known about it. Or why. What if this guy followed Memphis? What if you weren't the one being called and followed, but Memphis or Lila was? How would you feel if they wound up being killed because you didn't leave this to the police?"

I admit I didn't have a good response to that. I felt bad enough about what happened to Linda. I certainly didn't want anyone else getting hurt.

"Put an end to this, Jenevieve. I mean it."

I wasn't sure how I could, exactly, *"put an end to this."* There was still so much I didn't know about. Did we have enough for the police to take us seriously? Even if they did take it over, did that mean we were safe yet? It was hard going into work, knowing the place was the source of the craziness going on.

My family used to tell me when I applied to work at a bookstore that I could probably just sit in a corner and read all day, that it would be relaxing. I don't even get to relax and read at my book club. This wasn't what I had in mind at all, and yet I couldn't walk away. Someone looks at me weirdly at a coffee shop and I'll obsess over it all day, and yet here I was, pursuing a murder and finding out I've been drugged. How was I supposed to just drop everything and move on?

I tried to keep myself busy when I got to work so I didn't have to think about any of this anymore. Putting up stickers on spines of books according to genre, or rearranging displays–but I heaved a sigh of relief when I saw Elle coming in. *Perfect, somebody I can talk to who understands everything going on.* But when she got closer, I felt a hostile energy radiating from her. I stepped back, as if that energy could burn.

"Hey, what's going on? Did you hear any updates on your dad?"

Elle huffed. "Yeah. You could say that. How's this? My dad tried to kill himself. They found him foaming at the mouth. He had somehow gotten a bunch of pills and taken them. The world believes he's a criminal and he's afraid of prison, you do the math. He's in jail because of you guys!"

I blinked and took another step back. I was still too close to the fire and was now struggling to process the overload of information. He's in jail because of who now? "I'm sorry–what?"

"It's you! You gave us those stupid books, came up with the dumb idea to track down a ghost, and it warped my head! I never would have done anything like this if it wasn't for you. My father could have died!" Elle wiped her cheeks. "Thank God they found him in time..."

Flashbacks flooded my brain, reminding me of our childhood arguments. Calling me names, blaming me for stuff that wasn't my fault. But something was telling me these things didn't add up.

"Elle, please listen to me, I genuinely think there's something bigger going on. Lila and I were looking into the food we had at book club and somebody drugged us. Whoever did that to us, must've been the same to do that to your dad..!"

"We got drugged?!" Elle nearly shrieked. I gently pulled her to the side, trying to calm her down so bystanders wouldn't hear but she was uncontainable. "Why didn't you check the food you were serving?! Why am I just hearing about this now?!"

I flinched. "I...didn't want you to worry. Things were already difficult with your dad...I genuinely don't think he tried to kill himself, Elle..."

I reached for her arm, trying to comfort her but she slapped me away.

"Touch me one more time and see what happens! I'm not getting sucked into your world again."

Okay, that stung. I opened my mouth to reply, wanting to defend myself, but...I closed my eyes tightly and clenched my fists at my sides until they trembled. I desperately tried to contain the emotion threatening to bottle up. Elle was just upset. Her dad nearly died. I didn't want to argue with her. *Calm down.*

"I never should have come to these club meetings. You people live in a fantasy world. I don't know what I was thinking." Elle stomped to the door and slammed it behind her.

I thought things couldn't get any worse until I felt my phone buzz in my pocket. I sighed and reached to grab it, finding I got a text from my cousin that said,

Hey, just a heads-up, your mom told my dad about what we've been doing. He said he wants to meet with everyone :/

CHAPTER 20
TROUBLE

"In all my time serving this county, I have never heard of an idea more stupid." I wasn't sure if he was speaking as a captain or an uncle, but he was fuming either way.

We all sat in the room where it began. In the meeting room on the second floor, the stare from the paintings burning into my back as if Uncle Wyatt's face wasn't enough to unnerve me. If only everyone had taken this as well as my Pastor did.

The Carlyle programming space felt emptier than it had on the night of our first meeting. Just furniture and paintings. It was impersonal. What had been my art canvas almost a month ago, was now my interrogation room. I sat beside my fellow club members, feeling like I was getting chewed out by the principal. For a moment there, I thought we were doing some honorable thing by trying to help my coworker, but now we were being treated like juveniles.

We told him everything. Sneaking around the bookstore, investigating, meeting, and trading theories. We hadn't done anything illegal, so it wasn't like he could charge us for anything–Not that that did anything for his anger.

"When I told my son he was going to this club, it was because I wanted him to meet new people. The kind that would lead him away from trouble. Jenevieve Weston, my dear niece and goddaughter, has always–" He hesitated, "Has usually been a good example for him. Imagine my surprise when I get a call from your mother saying that you guys have been sneaking around, poking your nose into other people's business, and worst of all...putting yourselves in danger." Wyatt looked at me with brown eyes that belonged not to him but to an aging, wounded hound dog that had just been kicked off of a dirty rug he was sleeping on.

"You didn't seem so disappointed when I saved Jenevieve from robbers the other day," Memphis's defiance made me wince. He had a point, I'm sure everyone knew it, but the attitude he used to convey that sentiment was never going to win an argument against a parent, or an officer of the law. Unluckily for us all, Captain Wyatt Moses was both.

"There's a difference and you know it," my uncle hissed in return. "That burglary wasn't your fault. But when you go looking for trouble, you find it."

"Sir, we understand your concern, but we just wanted to prove that Linda's fall was worth looking into," James spoke up, to my surprise.

"Yeah, if you just believed us the first time, we wouldn't have done anything," Memphis added.

While the others were making a case, Lila brought out her phone, "Also, Captain Moses, I have evidence that shows that we were drugged? What should we have done about that?"

"First of all, you're not–" He paused, then leaned over to look at her phone. "Drugs?"

"See? We told you things were going on. And–" Memphis was about to go off but James held his hand out in front of him, silently warning him to stop while we were ahead.

"I didn't know anything about that stuff until today!" Elle held her hands up in defense, shaking her head some and pursing her lips.

"...Memphis?" Wyatt asked.

"Yeah, dad?"

"Tell me that you didn't do this." His question shook me. How did he jump to that conclusion??

"What?!"

"Well, right before book club, I found out you had been smoking in the bathroom with your friends. Now this just so happens to pop up."

I exchanged looks with the others. That thought had never entered my head for a second. Why would Memphis do something like that?

"Hugs, not drugs, Dad," Memphis folded his arms then a defiant smirk spread on his face. "But drugs do last longer."

"No–" James winced then shot him a look, "Please be serious with him."

Uncle Wyatt's face was growing increasingly red. Veins grew on the side of his neck. We were so dead.

"I told you I didn't smoke anything!" Memphis threw his hands up in the air, "Let me get something clear! Yes, I am a bad kid! I am a, 'crashed a dirt bike into a trash can' type of bad kid. Or hey, a 'breaking and entering' type of bad kid. I am NOT, 'roofied my cousin's book club' kind of bad kid!"

"Unfortunately, I wish I could believe that, Memphis, but your behavior has been so bad, I don't know what to think anymore." Wyatt pinched the bridge of his nose. "This discussion is not over. We'll dismiss today, but I'm going to want to speak to each of you—individually."

"Oh, don't worry," Elle narrowed her eyes at me, as if this wasn't directed at Wyatt, "I'm so done. With all of this."

"I'm so happy," my uncle replied, dejectedly. He snapped his fingers at Memphis and pointed to the door. Then the two of them left together.

Everyone rose silently from our chairs, collected our things, and followed their example. None of us had anything left to say to each other. Go, team. Despite having graduated last year, it felt like we just got out of detention. Why couldn't we be treated like adults? I ran a hand through my hair and tried to calm down. What an anti-climatic end to this whole adventure.

Amelia skipped up to me when I walked out, asking about the situation but drowning it in cheery words so she didn't come off as intrusive. It didn't work. "Hey, Jen-Jen! Is everything okay?"

My ex-club members breezed past, none of them murmuring a goodbye or even looking back at me. First was Memphis, then Elle, then Lila. *Wait, where's James?*

I turned to Amelia again and politely nodded. I didn't feel it necessary to mention everything. I did not have the strength for it. I wasn't in the mood to get chewed out for the third time today.

"Your uncle is here. Did you get into trouble?" asked Olive in a childish, taunting tone.

I pressed my lips together into a thin line, feeling the heat rising to my cheeks. I did not need this. I truly didn't. Then, over her shoulder, I saw James go in the direction of the door that the burglars had broken into. *Where is he going...?*

I turned my focus back on Olive, "I'm not being arrested so clearly, I'm not in trouble. But when I feel like updating you then I will."

"Ooh, someone's touchy," she reclined in her chair with a smirk. "It must be juicy if you're not telling us about it."

"Hey, hey. I don't like this negativity over here," Amelia interjected, "It's okay. Just...everyone, get back to work. Jen-Jen will let us know if she needs anything. Right, Jenny?"

I forced a smile and nodded again, murmuring an *'Mmhmm.'* As soon as I had an opportunity, I dipped out of that conversation. My shift was over, I didn't owe them anything. Wherever James was going, I had to follow.

I glanced over my shoulder one more time, relieved when my coworkers were busy and didn't see where we were going. In a paranoid impulse, I also looked up at the security cameras, making sure no one would catch it–serendipitously, the camera was perfectly angled away from that door. Convenient. Just when I thought it was perfect timing, I heard the front door open again. *Must be more customers.* Well, that was fine. I worked here, so as far as they knew, I was going into a staff-only area. I was all clear. I didn't look over my shoulder again when I went to follow the trail James left behind.

I took my first steps down the staircase, careful to be as quiet as possible. It didn't take me long to regret coming inside. I ducked just in time to miss a few cobwebs dangling overhead. The air went sour until all I could smell was must and the distinct stench of mold. It was like descending into a haunted maze. The dank and dark atmosphere making chills go down my back. Past what felt like a hundred steps, way past normal basement level. What caught my attention were the select spaces without dust. The steps below had noticeable rings around where they've been stepped through recently. Not just fresh prints like where James was going, but many, over time. This place wasn't as abandoned as we originally thought.

The deeper down I went, the darker it got. I was reminded of my nightmare. Barry Beaumont taunting me, how I'm that kid who didn't know how to leave stuff alone. I'd been given warning after warning, yet I found myself here. When I get out of this, I'm probably going to be sent straight to a psychiatrist. Maybe Elle was right about me. Normal people didn't do this. Although, I was following James. We must both be crazy.

I flinched when a light suddenly flashed on, seeing James using his cell phone to guide the way. It wasn't good that we were down here. We literally just got chewed out for doing this stuff.

I opened my mouth, taking a breath to warn him. Tell him to come out with me before we both get fired, but the words didn't come.

I thought I heard voices. But due to recent news, I wasn't sure if I could believe everything I saw or heard. Maybe it was just my imagination. I was proud of myself for not making loud footsteps. I was sure if I made just one wrong move then it would echo all throughout whatever this place was. The staircase seemed to stretch on forever, the light of day behind us getting fainter and fainter. When I looked back one more time, that's when I made that mistake I had predicted about. I had found the bottom of the stairs, tripping and falling forward when I felt a pair of strong arms catch me.

"Jen? What are you doing down here?!" a voice scolded me in a whisper.

When I regained my balance, I let go of James and backed away. "I could ask you the same thing."

"It's not safe. Go." I wasn't used to hearing him talk to me like this. He was using the voice he used on Memphis when he got in trouble. I used to think that voice made James sound all cool, but it wasn't fun being on the receiving end. Or seeing his brow furrow in disappointment in the dim gleam of his phone's flashlight, "Your uncle said to stop. Take his advice."

I folded my arms, gently rubbing them when I noticed how cold it was down here. "T-that goes both ways. If I shouldn't be down here, why are you?"

James fell silent for a moment. I'd seen that wounded expression once before, at Celia's. After a second or two, realization dawned on me and I softened.

"What happened to Linda wasn't your fault. You know that, right? You don't have to do this."

"Yeah, I do..." He muttered and turned his eyes away from my face, "It was my job to look after the building and I didn't. If I had just been awake, maybe Linda would be alive."

"But it's not your fault! The only one at fault here is whoever pushed her down those stairs!"

James threw his hands up in his agitation, "Then I have to find out whoever did!"

"Poor choice of words..." a new voice startled me.

I didn't know they had any lights down here that worked until they all came on in the blink of an eye. I realized just how much was waiting there in the dark when I saw a group of men surrounding us. Even our friends were down here. They must have done the same thing James and I did. So much for that promise we made to Uncle Wyatt. Lila, Elle, and Memphis were being held by their arms, even as they tried to struggle, but they didn't get very far.

"Let me go! Back off, man!" Memphis squirmed in one of the men's grip. Despite his protests, of course, he was not let go. The big bad dude who had hold of him didn't so much as blink, as if Memphis was just a toddler throwing a tantrum, a minor inconvenience to him.

The imagery was startling on its own but then I saw the man in the center of this mess. He stood there in a colorless hazmat suit and clear protective mask. So, that explains why we saw a monstrous white figure. The drugs made us see the ghost of Barry Beaumont, but when he took off his gas mask, we saw our chaser was my coworker all along. Andy Smith, the innocuous IT guy.

"Get them in room 5b. Just shove them in there until I figure out what to do with them," Andy told a couple of the men, who immediately followed his word and started walking towards us.

"Get back! Stay back!" James stepped in front of me then swung defensively at the men, trying to create distance.

One of the thugs grabbed his arm and yanked him forward, to our surprise. The security guard was quickly overpowered and his attacker stuck something in his neck. After a minute or two, the fight drained out of him and he fell limp–making me feel the sick realization we had never known what actual trouble looked like until now. I missed when we were just bickering over takeout in the meeting room.

"No!" I made a mad dash forward to help James but the other man grabbed me too, his fingers digging into my bicep. A short pinprick stabbed into me then everything went black within seconds.

CHAPTER 21
TRAPPED

"I wonder what they'll do to us..." Elle mumbled, her blank gaze set on the moldy carpet beneath us.

"Could be anything, really." Lila rubbed her swollen, red neck as she answered the rhetorical question. "Shoot us. Or maybe inject us with poison. Drugs seem to be their thing. Did you know if you inject air between the toes then it will look like the victim died of a heart attack?"

Elle shot her a dirty look.

"Sorry."

I sat in my little corner of the dusty, dark room with my head in my hands. Everything my mom and uncle said was right. I never should have done this. I'd had more than enough warnings, plenty of opportunities to turn back, yet I still went on with it. If only I'd gone at it alone, then I wouldn't be worried sick for the people around me. I got swept up in the fun of it all, sharing my childish idolization for Sherlock with what I wanted to call my friends. If they died, would their blood be on my hands? Was I a terrible person?

"I'm sorry too..." I weakly began but Elle interrupted me with a sharp,

"Don't start."

I blinked. "I'm just trying to–"

"I know. It's annoying. We all know it's your fault we're in this mess. No sense rubbing it in."

Lila glanced between us, "Is it really the time for this?"

"It looks like we got plenty of time to me." Elle's long fingernail directed us towards the door.

"And...now!" James ordered.

I felt the wall behind me shudder. The impact caused the single hanging light bulb over my head to bounce and flicker. James and Memphis tried to ram into the door to knock it down but it wouldn't budge. Both guys groaned and wobbled back, grabbing their hurting shoulders in unison.

"This door is impossible," James growled, eyeing his target with hatred.

"Is this what old people mean when they say things aren't built like they used to be?" Memphis quipped.

When it had fallen silent again, what Elle said started to nag at me. Actually, everything Elle has ever said to me. I was already beating myself up over this and her blame game wasn't helping. I probably should have let it go but instead I asked,

"You do realize I didn't plan for any of this, don't you? I never meant for any of this to happen."

"Maybe not this," Elle gestured around the small cement room before motioning between me and her, "But definitely this."

"Sleuthing wasn't just my idea."

"Oh yeah? Then why did you start apologizing if you don't think it's your fault we're here?" She folded her arms and shifted her weight, turning all her attention to me.

I laughed in disbelief. *Was she being serious?* She was utterly impossible. I turned away as if the peeling art deco wallpaper was much more worthy of my attention than this conversation.

"Can you quit turning into a little shrimp when you get scared? That's what's getting to me. You never stop the nice girl thing. Whether ghosts attack you or I do, you'd get hit in the face and still apologize." Elle laughed, though her voice held little humor.

It was strangely quiet on the other side of our room. Not even Memphis was trying to crack a joke. I almost wanted to see how everyone else was reacting, but was too scared to look. We'd be lucky if we survived this mess, yet we were having this conversation. Here, of all places.

Elle had really never changed, had she? I felt like I was on the playground at school again, getting taunted and called names. Back then we were just kids but she was choosing now to get on me again? In front of my friend, my cousin, and my crush?

"Jen—" Lila was a second too late.

"What do you want me to do?!" My voice cracked on the last word. My eyes were stinging so I glared up at the ceiling. I didn't care, I refused to cry in front of other people. "Huh? What do you want from me?"

Elle moved in closer, her eyes locked on me, planting her feet like a tree that wouldn't be moved. "Defend yourself! Was it worth it to start sleuthing or wasn't it? Are you just another victim here or what? Prove yourself to me. Prove it. Prove it's not your fault."

"I don't have to prove anything!" I met her eyes and tightened my jaw. My hands trembled by my sides so I balled them into fists. "I'm sorry about your dad, and I'm sorry about the circumstances that led us here, but…it's not my fault. We all agreed to quit, and still found ourselves here! Separately! You may think I'm crazy for the Sherlock stuff, but you're all just as crazy as me! Looks like none of us could stop if we tried! I've bent over backwards, I've tried everything, but I don't know what I can do to make you happy."

When my words' echoes stopped, the silence returned. It may have only been two seconds, but it was an eternity to me. That actually felt good. A little dizzying, but that was probably still the drug floating around in my system. Ever since this started, I've been trying to keep things friendly so we could all get along, but all I needed was to be sedated and kidnapped before I finally flipped my lid and released all the energy I've been wrestling with since Linda died.

"She did it. She's finally lost it." I heard Memphis whisper to James.

I lifted my glasses over my head and ran my hands down my face. Wiping away sweat and tears. When I slipped my glasses back, I looked back at Elle. I hoped the argument was over because I was exhausted after that.

Elle folded her arms and pursed her lips. She shifted her weight, pausing a moment, as if deciding how she was going to react to what I said. The side of her mouth twitched and the look in her eyes was indiscernible. After forever, she said, "I guess that'll do, for now."

Lila cleared her throat and laughed nervously. "How about we just focus on getting out of here...?"

I let out a shaky breath and nodded before looking around the room again, this time trying to think of anything I could find that could help our situation. As well as avoiding Elle's face. We could go to group therapy when we got out of here–God willing.

Was there any way to get help? Nobody knew we were down here. No one in the store even goes down here–other than Andy, apparently. Calling for help obviously wouldn't work. We were down past the basement, no one would hear us.

I reached for my neck, rubbing the itchy spot where they'd stuck me with that needle. I could still feel the effects as the drug slowly got out of my system. I was awake but everything was moving in slow motion. Or like someone had hit a reverb button in my brain. Whatever it was, it was way stronger than what Andy had given us at book club. Despite my fuzzy thinking, I put together that he must've done that while he was carrying my snacks up for me. I thought he was just being nice, but obviously not anymore.

"I-If only I had a box of matches..." I thought out loud, "I saw online that you can put ashes in the lock, put the wooden end of an unused match in, light the red part and when the fire hits the base, it unlocks..."

I turned back to the door with sudden excitement but all hope dissipated instantly, "...if only our captors locked the door on our side."

Elle rolled her eyes and scoffed.

"If we were trying to break in somewhere instead of out, that would be a good idea, Jen," James murmured supportively, "How did you know that?"

"I had hoped all that useless research would come in handy someday, but I don't think this is that day."

"It's a shame. I got some matches in my bag. I found this cute box of antique ones we got at the store the other day." Lila actually seemed to pout a little.

For the hundredth time since we'd been thrown in, there was that awkward silence again. It was a bad sign when this group could shut up all at the same time. That's how you know we're in trouble when we find something we can't bicker or laugh about.

I looked at the other members to see how they were hanging in there. James was leaning against the wall, rubbing his glassy eye with his knuckle, staring into space. His curly coffee hair was messy, pointing in every which direction. Elle lazily looked at her nails, checking for any damage that may have been done to her manicure during the scuffle. Memphis was like a tick about to pop, bouncing on his feet and sizing up the door as if he was thinking about ramming it again. I turned again to Lila, who was staring at the door. I thought she was just spacing out like James but then she spoke up,

"I think I got an idea." Lila started to grin. "Fun fact about me. I am the youngest of three prankster siblings. Who used to lock me in my room for grins and giggles. I had to get real creative about how to escape. Most of the time, I had to take out the hinges."

"Yeah, I'm real glad I didn't have your siblings growing up," Elle commented.

"That's actually really funny," Memphis snickered. It didn't surprise me that he found the humor in it. It sounded like something he'd do if he had a younger sibling.

I shot him and Elle a look then tried to avoid their commentary, "That's a great idea, Lila!"

"Yeah, I wish I'd thought of it," James agreed.

"Eh, I'm sure you would have. If we weren't panicking and...a little high right now." Lila let out a squeaky nervous laugh before motioning the guys over for their help.

I couldn't believe I'd just stumbled into a lifelong friendship with a genius, lucky me.

While she, James, and Memphis worked on the door, my eyes wandered over to Elle. Even though everything she said hurt, I still felt bad for her. Why have we always been at odds with each other? I've known her so long, I couldn't even think of when this all began. I just wanted to be on cordial terms with her and move on with our lives.

"Don't look at me like that. Stop it." Elle snapped without even looking back at me.

"What am I doing now?"

"We're not having a moment. I just want out of here."

I sighed in defeat and focused back on the door, trying to respect her wishes. To my surprise, she spoke again,

"I'll ask you something though if you promise just to answer once and drop it."

I immediately spun around to her again.

"Why do you keep trying to make nice with me? Even after I've insulted you in every way I can think of?"

Her question made me pause. I wasn't entirely sure myself. I was trying to be like Jesus. Maybe I was a people-pleaser. Maybe the drugs wearing off were messing with my emotions. I wasn't the one who figured out how to get the door open, but I wanted to look out for everybody in any way I could. All that was a little too much to answer with so I tried to make a joke,

"My mom always said to kill people with kindness?"

"Could you do me a favor then?"

"Hmm?"

"Next time, smother me with a pillow," Elle said. "That would be much better than being stuck down here in this sewer hole."

Not entirely sure if she was being playful or not, I forced out a laugh. I think this was the closest I would be getting to a resolution. If there was any sign that she and I were okay, maybe that was it. Thankfully, I didn't have to sit with my thoughts for much longer, because the others managed to get the door to open.

"We got it! We got it!" Memphis pumped his fists up in celebration.

His volume made James shoot him a look. "Say it louder–I don't think they heard you."

"Oh, sorry. I mean–oh no! The great power of this door is too much!" Memphis held a hand to his heart and gave a groan of dramatic despair, I think solely to make the vein on the side of James's temple threaten to pop out.

"Just shut up, man..."

I don't think it made a difference in the end whether we were quiet or not because when we all got out, there were three men guarding our door out in the hall. I was hoping this would be like a movie and we could just sneak out of here.

"Get the syringes! Use a stronger dose this time!" A man barked at his shorter friend.

Said shorter friend turned to a bag where I assumed the syringes were kept but thankfully, Memphis didn't waste any time. He tackled him to the ground, making it more difficult to get to the drugs. That's when the fight broke out. While Memphis handled that guy, James and I took on the tall man with tattooed sleeves while Elle and Lila went against a middle-height blonde guy with a nose piercing.

Tall tattoo man swung at James, making the latter duck. James dove behind him and took hold of his waist, controlling his torso before ordering me to get him. I kicked our captor in his gut until he keeled over, giving James time to pick up one of the folded chairs they had been sitting on and hit him in the face with it, knocking him out.

Elle and Lila pushed their blonde guy into the room we were in, using the chair and tall guy's body to keep him shut up in there. Just when we thought we were winning, we turned to see the short guy elbowed Memphis away from him and got the bag with the drugs in it–and none of us liked that so we went at him. This part is a bit of a blur to me, I was still a little out of it and the adrenaline was high so the details are fuzzy here but eventually we overpowered him. Memphis got one of the syringes and stabbed the remaining guy with it. Then we all took off down the hall. Playing a serious game of hide n' seek from any remaining of Andy's thugs.

We had been trying to find the exit but the first room we came across was an office. A shady, dark, and suspicious looking one. Made out of a room like the kind we'd escaped from with old carpet and peeling wallpaper but it had a small table and a laptop resting on it.

"These guys got cozy down here, didn't they?" James blinked.

"You think this is Andy's?" I was curious what was on it but I also really just wanted out of here before we got caught again.

"I dunno. Let's check it out." Memphis clearly didn't share my concerns because he was wandering over to the table and opening the laptop. The rest of us, predictably, followed.

"I'm surprised an IT guy doesn't have better security for his laptop in his secret base of operations…" Lila said as we scrolled through his emails for anything we'd like to know before we went straight to the police. Andy might delete everything once we get out of here.

"This is probably the one place he felt safe to leave his work.." I murmured. Until us, I don't think he had, "guests."

James tapped suddenly on the screen, "Hey, up here. Who is M?"

Memphis clicked on the last email Andy sent. The message read,

> M,
>
> Looking forward to meeting you face-to-face. I have heard a lot about your work and I am a huge fan. Hope my work is pleasing to you and begins a lucrative future for both of us.
>
> Sincerely, Andrew Beaumont

"Andrew Beaumont? You think that's Andy's real name?" Memphis asked then made a face, "Smith is such a basic name. I can't believe he chose that for his fake one. It's so obvious."

"Well, it worked for him." Lila shrugged.

"Wait a minute. Andrew Beaumont?" The cogs in my head began to turn., "That was the name of Barry Beaumont's son. Is that just a coincidence or is Andy descended from the guy we thought was haunting us?"

"Who cares?!" Elle threw up her hands, "Whether his great-grandpa was the president or a janitor, I just want to go!"

"Wait, wait. We still don't know who M is..." James turned the computer in his direction and scrolled through the email, his brows knitted in focus.

"Hey, guys! I found our phones!" Memphis opened up a drawer in the desk that had our stuff in it, all in a plastic bag.

"Great! Get some pictures of these emails so we can show your dad." Lila pointed towards the computer until Elle got her cell and did what Lila suggested.

"It looks like he has a buyer set up soon. Think this will be enough to get Andrew or Andy or whoever he is, in trouble?" I looked around at the others with hope, "This email, our testimonies, and pictures of the tunnels?"

"Could be." James pressed his lips together, "But I'd like to be absolutely sure. I do know the process would take too long. By the time we find out how much evidence we need, this deal will already be settled and Andy might leave Ohio for good. Taking everything with him."

Once we had our stuff back and we'd taken whatever photos we could, we managed to find the exit and get out of the bookstore. For once in our whole investigation, we finally went to the police to tell them what we knew instead of trying to handle this ourselves. Only problem was, it didn't take us long to regret that choice.

CHAPTER 22
TRAPPED, AGAIN

I wish someone had a camera when we all barged into the Waxwood Police Department...again. All sweaty, our hair ragged, grimy from being in that stupid basement. The basement of a basement, even. We'd been drugged, locked away, accosted, faced a murderer, and all in the span of a few hours. All eyes were on us from every officer when we came in, but no one made a move to approach us yet.

There was a familiar face at the desk already but I hadn't noticed him until Elle cried, "Daddy!" She threw herself into his arms, squeezing him tight.

Then my uncle came round, "What's going on here? You guys look terrible. Where have you been?"

Despite being winded, Memphis had enough breath to quip, "We'd like to report a crime..."

They moved us to a conference room so we all could talk about what happened privately. They were unamused, to say the least, that our oath to never sleuth again hadn't lasted long.

"I was afraid something like this would happen. I wasn't sure if it was Andy necessarily, but I knew something was going on," Gonzales shook his head. Without looking up, he reached over for his daughter and comfortingly rubbed her arm.

"Not that it's any of y'all's business," Wyatt cleared his throat, "But we just had a very interesting conversation about those burglars, you remember. You didn't have to go looking into this. Gonzales here was trying his hardest to find out what Andy was doing. If you hadn't knocked out his investigators..."

"You mean that thing I got a hearty, 'atta boy' for a few days ago?" Memphis cocked a brow. "They were good guys?"

"I wanted to keep it quiet," Gonzales sighed. "But we've been able to clear that misunderstanding. Like he said, though, none of you had to get into this. Especially you, Elle."

I blinked in confusion. I couldn't believe those shady guys I'd overheard were legit. Or even semi-legit. They were basically cartoon characters–no offense...to them.. They'd probably think the same of us. If we hadn't interfered then would they have found out about what was going on in the tunnels?

I glanced over at Lila but she mirrored my confusion, her eyes narrowed with doubt as we listened to all of this.

"Alright, then you have what you need to arrest him now?" James leaned back in his seat and folded his arms, his brow subtly twitching. "I would think we have more than enough evidence."

Whatever emotions were stewing in my uncle suddenly faltered. He opened his mouth but nothing came out.

"You don't need to wait for a warrant or anything. I give you full permission to enter the building if that's what you need," Gonzales offered.

"It's not that. I'm just concerned once he finds out you kids escaped, he'll have the place swept clean by the time we get there," Uncle Wyatt scrubbed a hand over his salt and pepper goatee, scratching pensively at the chin.

"He has a big deal coming up," I blurted. "With someone important."

"Yeah! We took pictures of the emails if you want to see..." Elle started to bring out her phone but her dad gave her a look and motioned for her to put it away.

"That doesn't matter. You've already been told to quit looking into these things and I meant it. Not to step on your toes, Mr. Gonzales, but I'm pretty positive he agrees with me that your part in this is done. This is a police investigation now. You wanted our attention, you got it." My uncle got up from the table, the discussion part over with. "I'm gonna get you stupids over to some medical help, get you checked out, all that fun stuff. Then we're gonna make sure you don't play Nancy Drew anymore."

Memphis scoffed, "What are you going to do? Lock us up?"

They did, in fact, lock us up.

Half an hour later, we all found ourselves in a holding cell. I didn't know if this was legal, if we were being charged with anything–I doubted it. I really wished Memphis hadn't opened his mouth because this was the second time today–tonight? That we were being held in a tiny room against our will. Except instead of a Prohibition tunnel spare room, we were in a painted brick room, sitting behind bars. Actual bars. I thought that was just in movies. My cousin was making the best of it though; he had been trying to stick his arm through and get the door, but it was, of course, locked.

"You'll never take us alive!" Memphis announced to the entire jail.

"I think it's too late for that, man..." James rested his head against the wall and closed his eyes for a moment. His dark circles underneath were darker than usual.

"I know, I just wanted to say that." Memphis shook the bars one last time out of pettiness before turning around.

"I cannot believe my dad agreed to him shoving me in here." Elle sniffed the air then gagged. She looked down at the metal bench Lila, James, and I sat on then wrinkled her nose, shaking her head like that wasn't an option for her. She instead paced along the opposite wall, wrapping her hair up in her usual bun with a scrunchie,

"I think we've been through enough for one day. Yet they throw us in here like some common criminals."

"I can't blame him. I wouldn't trust us either," Lila shrugged. "I think we beat the world record for fastest order defied. Literally just told us to stop sleuthing, then we turned around and...yeah."

"Look, I was upset earlier when I said you all warped my head and blah, blah. But that is actually kind of true because I'm weirdly addicted to this investigating stuff now..." Elle sighed, sounding less frustrated with me and more at the situation now. That was a good sign.

"I just hope they get this taken care of," I murmured and shook my head. "They had better catch him. And whoever his buyer is. Do you believe they would have caught him with the investigators if we hadn't interfered?"

"I don't believe that for a second," Memphis scoffed. "Those guys were easily taken down by a ghost story. There were only two of them and a basement full of drug dealers. "We may have just saved the morons' lives."

Lila nodded in agreement, "Yeah, and then Andy would've packed up and moved. Remember what they tried to do to Gonzales while they were talking to him–sorry, Elle."

"I'm just glad he's okay." Elle held up a hand, reassuring us that we were okay on that front, now that he was cleared of any suspicion and wasn't actively being poisoned anymore. Wow, she got over things quicker than I thought she would. It had been a long day for all of us, though. Maybe we were getting that "war buddy" camaraderie.

My knee bobbed wildly where I sat. *Were they going to be too late? How were they going to go about this? Would they spook the buyer? What if Andy had more connections?*

Uncle Wyatt was probably right to lock us up. Now that we were hooked on this, it was really difficult to turn off that part of your brain that was constantly asking questions and wanting to know where everything was going. But it looked like we were, officially, benched.

"Welp, my friends, how are we escaping this time?" Memphis clapped his hands together then looked over the bars. "Do we want to take off the hinges again? Although I doubt that will work here. These doors are different."

My brows suddenly lifted. I glanced at the others and then looked down at the floor. I decided I wasn't saying anything. I would not be accused of leading the group into danger again. I refused.

James looked up at Memphis. "Do we really want to do that? That would be a *jailbreak*, you realize that, right? An actual crime. This isn't like earlier."

Memphis held up a hand and started counting, "Number 1, my dad is the police captain. And 2, I don't think we're even *lawfully* being kept here."

"Good point."

I looked around, afraid of what would happen if somebody heard us. Although, most of the cops would be on the Andy case, or on the outside of those doors and they were all friends of ours. I suppose it was a good gamble–but I shook my head and sank in my seat, folding my arms. *Nope. Not putting my two cents in. Nope.*

"Come on, guys. Are you with me? We've made it so far—we're going to leave this with them? That's no fun." Memphis stuffed his hands into his pockets and rocked on his heels childishly, "We're a team, aren't we? Lila? I see that look in your eyes. You think this is fun too. And Elle? Come on, princess, don't tell me you're still mad."

"Oh yeah, I'm mad," Elle made a face, looking up at him and pursing her lips for a moment. "At the guy who poisoned my dad. Drugged us. Locked us up in his moldy room. That was personal."

"Exactly," Memphis motioned towards her and nodded eagerly. "Thank you. Now, do we want to let my dad have all the fun? They don't even know what they're doing. They don't know the place like we do. They were wrong about the investigators, they're wrong about this. Who is with me?"

Lila hummed for a moment then nodded. "I'm in."

"As soon as I get the chance, I'm kicking that IT nerd in the shin," Elle agreed.

James chuckled. "I guess I don't have anything to lose."

I raised a brow, waiting for them all to look at me but they didn't wait for my consent. The four of them just congregated by the door and glanced around, trying to decide the best way to get out of this cell. They talked about calling one of the police and rationalizing with them, asking for a phone call or some water. They noticed the regular lock on the front of the door and how they could slip their hands through the bars without a problem. It was easy to see this room was just for smaller cases until criminals would be transported. Waxwood hasn't been as fun in the criminal department until recently.

"I have a knife, maybe I can use that as a tool." Lila dug into her bag then suddenly froze.

Suspense hung in the air for five seconds before Lila slowly pulled her arm out, revealing the matches she had talked about in our last prison.

This was the moment everyone turned to me.

"No." I crossed my arms with a huff.

"Jenevieve..." Lila began with a sing-song voice.

"I said no."

"Oh, come on," Elle whined, much to my surprise. "You're the Sherlock geek here. You're the one with the fun facts and book research and whatever." She had just accused me of taking everyone into a fantasy world and now they were begging me to do this. "Show us what you were talking about earlier."

"I'd do it myself but I have a bad memory when it comes to instructions..." Memphis drew out that last word like his voice was getting farther away.

I shook my head stubbornly then adjusted my glasses. "Mm-mm. Nope. I've had enough people tell me lately that I've been leading you guys to the slaughter. I'm not gonna do it again. I don't want you guys to get hurt and let it be because of me. We told the police, we did our part, we're done."

There was a collective sigh and the four of them murmured amongst themselves what they were going to do. There were some head nods and subtle gestures until they all spoke up, overlapping each other.

"You wanna be Sherlock, be Sherlock–"

"I believe in you."

"We're not gonna die."

"I'm sorry I said that, okay? Come help us."

I cocked a brow, unmoving.

James looked around at the others before turning to me again. "This is for Linda."

Now that got me. I looked down at my feet and reached for my lip, picking at it while I weighed the pros and cons. I was so tired. Of the running around, of arguing, of literally being threatened and kidnapped...but James did have a good way of grounding me to the root of what we were doing. We were all young, but we weren't children. We didn't even choose to be in the middle of this, really. We were brought into it when Andy drugged us and killed Linda. She deserved justice and her family deserved the truth.

So, I swallowed my pride and got up before coming over to the bars. Lila handed me a couple matches as they all stood back to watch me work. My slim wrist went through the bars and I rubbed off the grounds from the end of the first match, until they fell into the lock. I lit the second match and stuck the wooden end inside the lock. The flame lowered down to the end, to the lock where the grounds were–and then there was a click.

Why did I always let them talk me into these things?

CHAPTER 23
OUR LAST BOW

Once we left the holding area, those still in the police station hardly noticed us exit the building. At the end of town, there was an abandoned railroad tunnel. We discovered it when we escaped Andy just a few hours ago, some place most people thought was condemned until we'd discovered it. Now we'd go in the way we left. If anybody had a plan, they didn't share it with me. Everyone just talked about how excited they were to see the end of this. To see Andy get arrested, to see this big bad "M" guy that he was emailing.

As I got a whiff of the odors of chemicals and mold, my anxiety at being down here the first time all flooded back. Along with glitching memories of my nightmares, telling me, maybe warning me to leave well enough alone. Beaumont's crumbling statue, holding me as I watched my friends all about to be destroyed. How helpless I was to save them. It was my call that brought us back to these tunnels, what if we didn't make it out this time?

My heart stopped when I heard shouting at the opposite end of our wing of the hideout. The announcement of the police's presence and the order to put their hands up. There was yelling and to our surprise, even gunfire, causing us to flinch and unconsciously huddle closer like a family of frightened raccoons.

"Over here!" James motioned us towards a pile of crates we could hide behind.

"Don't open it up, Lila, remember how well that went for us last time?" Elle eyed our friend.

"I'm a scientist. Scientists get curious," Lila retorted but they both got shushed by James.

Looking back on that last time, remembering the cloud of dust that formed when Lila opened the boxes...I don't think that was a cloud of dust. That explains the second time we hallucinated a ghost.

I prayed in my head that we would make it out of this okay. There was no reason for us to be here after all, we could see that, right? Did we have to see Andy get arrested just to feel closure?

James had said this was for Linda, but I couldn't help but feel this wasn't for Linda, but for us. For me. It was my call that got us out of the cell. Now we just had to hope we didn't die.

Suddenly we heard frantic footsteps. Someone was running. Getting closer. Was this coming down our hall? This wasn't closure. This wasn't the impartial third-party observer thing I had wanted.

"Ooh that's Andy." Memphis leaned over the crate then turned back to us, "Do you dare me to tackle him right now?"

"What? No!" I shot him a warning look.

"Did he slip past the police?" James whispered and went to get a peek too, "He's going to get away."

Memphis's eyes lit up, "I could catch him."

Of course he'd say something like that. Still treating this like a game of capture the flag or something, as if we were kids on the playground and not dumb young adults trying to take on a drug cartel.

"Memphis, don't do that..." Lila shook her head. "We're pushing it as it is by being here."

"Yeah, what if he has a weapon?" I hissed.

"Hmm, maybe let him go..." Elle quipped behind me. I couldn't believe she had a sense of humor right now in this situation. At least, I hoped she was joking.

James was quiet for a moment like he was weighing the options before sighing and shaking his head, "Don't, Memphis. Stay here."

"Eh, we've made it this far, right?" Memphis sent us a wink with a click of his tongue before jumping over the crate.

No matter how many times he pulled stunts like this, it never failed to nearly give me a heart attack. We all reached to hold him back but when Andy came running past our crate, Memphis tackled him. The two rolled around on the ground for a while, the criminal grunting and trying to shove my cousin off. He reached towards his belt and, just like I said...

He held out a handgun, "Get back! Don't touch me! Get...get on your knees! Hands behind your head!" Game over.

Memphis tightened his jaw, as if the command was more offensive than the weapon in his face. He met Andy's gaze and glared at him with all the defiance he could muster, but he did what he was told.

The rest of us were unsure what to do. Has he seen us yet? We all shuffled out of our spots, surrounding him in a circle. We didn't know what we were doing. Did we run? Did we try to wrestle him for the gun?

"You tried to kill my dad..." "...the police are here and they're going to take you in." "...if you miss, the bullet could ricochet and hit somebody." "...You're only going to make things worse for yourself." Everyone's dialogue overlapped with each other and echoed throughout the tunnel.

"Shut up! All of you!" Andy spun around, his eyes darting at each and every one of us as we unconsciously surrounded him. Wait a second, did we have the upper hand? Did he because he had a gun or did we because there were more of us than him? He could shoot somebody but then the rest of us could tackle him right after. I didn't know how many bullets he had in the chamber, had he used any when the cops came?

The sweat beading around his forehead, his panting breath fogging up his equipment goggles hanging loosely around his neck. Andy was caught and he knew it. His business was being reduced to ashes, his connections were gone. We were at an impasse.

Blurting out, I asked, "W-what happened to your deal? Did the police get your contact too?"

Anger flared in Andy's eyes in the low lighting, "M never showed. Not that it should matter to you." he held up his weapon towards me. A thought occurred to me now, what did it matter if you knew the truth, if you were too dead to share it? The way he glared me down, I could envision him as the Beaumont from my nightmares. The one crumbling, limited, desperate, and with the same gleam of murderous intent in his gaze.

"Jenevieve..." I heard James murmur.

I gulped, holding up my trembling hands as nausea kicked in. Two sides of me were warring, the side that wanted to be safe and logical, then the other side of me that was just tired. This guy had nearly killed me, nearly killed my friends, and he had killed Linda. I've faced a murderous fake ghost, burglars, a drug dealer's gang. I've been given drugs against my will, survived a car chase, only to find myself in this situation. I'm so tired of being scared. God got me through all that, if it was His will, He'd keep me here.

"How...how did you get Olive to agree to this? I-I know she's a hippie but getting into drugs is, uh, a little too stereotypical, isn't it? Aha..." I remembered something I heard from a Sherlock show once, *'people don't like giving information but they love to correct you when you're wrong.'* I wanted to test how right this was as I procrastinated getting murdered.

"What—Olive isn't part of this!" Andy snapped, "She's just—she's separate from all of this! She has nothing to do with this!"

Elle suddenly spoke up next, "Aww, you just thought she was pretty. Not exactly Bonnie and Clyde though, huh?"

"Stop talking!" Our enemy growled, but he lowered his voice, eyeing the opening past us as if he expected police to arrive at any time. He started shuffling along, in an attempt to make a run for it but we all stepped one bit closer.

No matter how many times Andy tried to get us to stop, he couldn't. Better men than him have tried. We kept popping up like popcorn. Asking questions, throwing them at him, talking over each other. What I used to think was our greatest weakness was now becoming a strength. We were relentless and overwhelming.

I think the adrenaline was getting to all of us. Keeping us up and up, but my spirits flipped from excitement to fear back and forth like a five year old playing with a light switch. Wondering how this was going to play out.

"I still can't believe your name is really Beaumont," Memphis guffawed. "Are you related to the magician dude?"

"My great-grandfather," Andy muttered.

"Didn't he die? Does that count?"

He let out a shuddering, humorless laugh and reached to wipe the perspiration off of his forehead, "He didn't really die.

He was an escape artist, moron. Did these tunnels not make you suspicious? These have been here since the building was a hotel! We traded alcohol! Or, they, uh, they did. Barry and his friend who owned the hotel. They nearly got caught. So, heh, Barry faked his death and went underground."

"Wow, that is so cliche." Elle rolled her eyes. "How long did that even last once Prohibition ended?"

"Heh. Well, when war came around, people started getting interested in stronger stuff..." The side of Andy's lips twitched into a smirk. He thrust his arms out, motioning wryly at the tunnels around us, "Feast your eyes on the family business! Hah...it dies with me. Four generation family business. Name changes, palms greased..aha...they wanted to move once the building became a bookstore, but I fought so hard to keep the original location..."

We finally grew quiet once he started rolling on his own. Classic villain monologue. Tensions were rising, his time was short. He was cracking.

"I got a job here. Made a life here. Had to keep turning Gonzales the other way. Health conditions, I said. Nothing of interest down there, I said. It just kept going! Then that stupid old lady! It's like ingrained in them to be nosey. No big deal, just get rid of her. Old ladies have accidents all the time. Then you guys came to the scene!"

"You drugged us..." I muttered.

"Drugged me," James's voice got darker.

"Normally I don't conduct work matters on bookstore hours but I had to. This was supposed to be the most important deal of our business...but you..." Andy looked around at us again, laughing humorlessly again, "What are you guys? The Scooby gang or something? I'm done. But you know what? So are you." When he lifted his weapon once again, there was a collective gasp. It was aiming right for me again.

"Jenevieve!"

"Jen, no!"

The others's voices overlapped again.

I liked this better than my nightmares. Once he shot me, the others would have time to escape. I lowered my surrendering hands and took a deep breath. Accepting the situation for what it was, and just waiting for the impact. I closed my eyes and...

Bang.

Wait, where was the pain? Was it the shock? Did it get me in the head, was I dead yet? I opened my eyes, stunned when I saw Andy. He was on the ground, groaning and writhing as a crimson puddle slowly pooled beneath him.

"They're over here!" My uncle's voice made me want to jump for joy. He hurried to my side, his gun smoking from the shot he fired. "Are you alright? Tell me! Are you alright?!"

With his foot, James hooked Andy's gun and kicked it far away from the rest of us while he was down. If Andy survived that, he'd have an impressive scar to show off in prison.

I nodded shakily. "Yeah, yeah. I think I'm alright."

"Are you crazy?!" "Why didn't you shut up?!" "I thought I was supposed to be the crazy one!" "Don't ever do that again!" "We got the bad guy!" "Can I kick Andy in the shin real quick?"

The others gathered around me, doing that thing where they talked over each other again but it was at twice the speed this time, everyone getting their nervous jitters out when it was safe again.

"I could've sworn I locked you kids up..." my uncle muttered as he bent down to cuff Andy and make sure he stayed subdued when they got him medical attention. "Do you guys have some secret marines training I don't know about?"

A nervous laugh bubbled out, "No! No. I don't know. I guess we just got lucky."

No, it wasn't luck, actually. I know there's a God because I've been pushing this situation for almost a month and it didn't get me killed. Thank the good Lord. Thank God.

"Don't tell me you're going to get mad again, Dad," Memphis whined. "We just got you a drug dealer and a murderer."

"We'll talk about this when we get home." Uncle Wyatt shot his son a look, then he softened and there was a gentle twinkle in his eye. "For now, let's just get you to the paramedics. Again."

"Heh, I think we're wearing him down," Elle smirked.

Memphis let out a whoop and threw his fists up in the air, signaling victory. Then he lowered his hands and opened his palms, giving us a little smirk until we high-fived him. There were a lot of hugs and relieved laughter, all our fear defeated and replaced with nothing but pure celebration.

I couldn't believe it. We did it. Around a month's work of sticking our noses where they don't belong. Everything finally clicked.

The paramedics took Andy away on a stretcher. The guy was still groaning and in pain while Memphis took Elle's hands and yanked her into a rushed mixture of a salsa and a waltz, the two of them muttering a song under their breaths, doing their little victory dance.

Uncle Wyatt shook his head and chuckled at us, "Yeah, enjoy it while you can. You're still in so much trouble."

None of us took him seriously. How could we? I swayed on my feet, unsure if I was going to throw up or faint. I leaned on Lila for support, throwing a loose arm in a sort of hug while we both just laughed at each other. Even James was smiling. He wasn't slap happy like the rest of us, but he wore a sort of peace on his features. We did it.

EPILOGUE

"Andy recovered from the wound. A mercy from God. When I saw the blood, I thought for sure he wouldn't..." I began, but when my eyes wandered over to James, he just shook his head and I changed the subject, "His court stuff won't start for a while, but they're confident he'll be put away for a long time. He confessed, so now that they know where to look, they're finding more evidence against him of what he did. Both with the drugs and your, uh, and your mom."

James reached over, his hand resting on my arm in a way that made my heart flutter. Even if he was just warning me to shut up. I took another sip of my tea, looking up into Celia's features, searching for any signs of disbelief or anger. Her jaw was slack and her eyes were wide, her only visible emotion being shock.

"You're saying...you guys really did all that?" Celia's voice was barely above a whisper. "For my mom?"

"We did it for you too!" I took my final sips of the tea she made me then set the mug down on a doily coaster. "Your mom was a hero. She knew something was wrong and when she found out what it was, she went immediately to tell the police. She was doing the right thing. So, uh, now you know the truth."

"If this didn't line up with what the police told me then I would've thought you were crazy..." She ran a hand through her graying brown hair. Her eyes fell to the carpet for a moment, "I don't know what to say."

"Your mom was a good woman." James said, "She deserved the effort put into finding what happened to her."

"Thank you both so much. Also, thank...thank your friends for me..." Celia sniffed then wiped at her cheek before looking up again, smiling brightly. The way the light shone on her and the way her eyes were turned up, it was like I was talking to Linda herself. When I blinked, the vision was gone. Hopefully she was in a better place, and God let her see this moment.

We exchanged hugs but before I could follow James out the door, Celia gently pinched the end of my sweater, pulling me back so she could softly say, "You know...heh, that would make an incredible book. The story you just told me."

I furrowed my brows as it took a moment to process her suggestion. My brows suddenly shot up again, "Really? You'd be okay with me doing that?"

Celia looked away for a moment. She shrugged nonchalantly before turning away to close the door behind her, smirking as she did. *Oh no, that was so cryptic.* It's not like the idea of writing about this hadn't occurred to me, of course it had. I wouldn't be a writer if I hadn't thought about it. Being like Watson, our Boswell, sharing the crazy story we'd experienced for ourselves. I had book research to last a lifetime. Could I really do it?

I hurried after my friend, "James! James, do you think she was officially giving me permission? Or was it just a flippant comment? What do you think that means? James!"

"'*Sherlock Wannabes Solve Small Town Mystery*,'" Elle read off of her phone.

"Looks like we're heroes or something now."

I was so relieved to be back in the Carlyle Room. It didn't need any decorations this time. I was content with the wooden bookcases, the rain gently pattering on the windows, and even the smiling faces of Mr. and Mrs. Carlyle resting on top of the mantle. I was worried that I'd never look at this building the same way again. Maybe part of that was true. Now it was our victory hall. We'd conquered the biggest mysteries of this place and rid the world of all the horrible things the Beaumont family line did. We were finally safe.

Elle was about to set down her phone but another notification soon dinged. Whatever message she got caused her brows to lift with interest. She smirked. Her eyes drifted off her phone and toward...my cousin across the table, who was stuffing his own device into his pocket. *What was that little exchange? What was that?*

I opened my mouth to pry but Memphis interrupted, "I can't believe there's no reward for helping the police..." He took his chopsticks and used them to shove a bunch of noodles into his mouth while he kicked his feet up on the table, only rolling his eyes when I swatted at his shoes, trying to get his feet down again.

"I think our reward is not being locked up again," I pointed out. "My mom was in hysterics when she finally heard everything. My dad took it a lot better. I think it helped that he found out after the fact. They've already threatened *dire* consequences if I ever did anything like it again."

James scoffed. "As if we'd get the chance again."

"Maybe it's for the best," Lila shrugged. "We've had enough excitement."

"Well, I for one, want–no–*need* more excitement." Memphis frowned, swallowing another bite of his noodles. "When's the next one? What's next? Local vampire? Werewolf?"

"*Hound of the Baskervilles*?" I suggested. "That was kind of like what we went through...kind of...in a way. We can always read about it." I then laughed, "I'm just kidding. The next book after *A Study in Scarlet* is the *Sign of Four*. We have a couple short story compilations to go until we hit the *Baskervilles*."

There was a collective groan at the table. Everyone, except for Lila, was disappointed–and I couldn't say I blamed them. It was hard going back to reading about adventures when you just got done living them for yourself. Nonetheless, I took out the box and opened it up before pushing everyone's copies to them.

"You know, I never actually signed up for a book club..." James murmured as he picked up his book, thumbing his way through the pages, probably grateful it was a short one.

"Yet you still come to our meetings." I sent him a teasing look. Reaching under the table, I pulled out one last box. "I do have one more thing for you guys. To commemorate our time together. It's not a cash reward like Memphis was hoping for, but..."

I passed out some gift-wrapped goodies. One for every member. Including myself. Not that I didn't already have a couple of my own but...

"Ooh it's one of those old thingies detectives use in movies!" Elle held hers to her eye and looked through the glass.

"A magnifying glass," I gently corrected.

"I wonder how the resale value on this would be," Memphis looked over the antique. When he saw my face then he immediately laughed, "I'm kidding! This is actually kinda cool, Jen. Thanks."

THE HOLMESIAN BOOK CLUB

"Hey, I helped her pick these out. We saw them at the antique shop." Lila smiled, "So if we ever do get into a situation like this again, we'll be ready."

Once everyone had their books and their gifts, we all sat down and dug into our meals. I noticed a fortune cookie beside my drink; I normally waited on those until after I finished my dinner but this time, I couldn't help myself. I got the cookie out of the wrapper, broke it in half then read the note inside:

"*Your best adventures are ahead of you.*"

Miss Weston,

I'm glad to inform you that we here at Mint Publishing are very impressed with your last submission. I see a great improvement here and we would be delighted to publish it for you. Congratulations.

I only have a couple of notes. I think it's a little whimsical. I have a hard time believing that a bunch of teenagers could solve a ghost story. It is a little Hardy Boys or Nancy Drew, if you ask me. Luckily, the characters are diverse enough. Did you take inspiration from a real group? You made yourself the main character, but I can't fathom the idea of you and your friends

solving mysteries. You're lucky the
characters are so charming. Great
improvement.

P.S. I was wondering if you were
interested in doing a sequel. There are a few
questions I'd like to see answered. Get back
to me.

Sincerely,
Michael Mint

ABOUT THE AUTHOR

JL Cordonnier is a Christian fiction writer who loves everything related to her literary hero, Sherlock Holmes. She would probably be just what Sir Arthur Conan Doyle would have hated. But he's to blame for her crusade to write stories just like him, about spectacular and peculiar people who fight to take down crime. Her debut mystery series, *The Holmesian Book Club*, illustrates her personal devotion to her craft and faith while paying homage to all of the fictional sleuths who preceded the lovable Jenevieve Weston.

THIS PUBLICATION WAS BROUGHT TO YOU BY:

A SUPPORTIVE PLATFORM FOR STORYTELLERS AND PEDDLERS ALIKE.

Being a creator by nature has its challenges, sharing those creations while keeping financially afloat being one of them. At Artisan Bards, we love nothing more than providing a safe and creative place for art, stories, and craftsmanship to live and flourish. We aim to build a mutually beneficial environment where each and every member has their creative needs met. Whether it's providing a basic landing page for a portfolio, crafting a digital environment for lore, or coaching you through the publication process of your well-written tales—we've got your back.

For more information on our services or to join our community, visit
www.artisanbards.com.